Scribe Publications
LIKE A HOUSE ON FIRE

Cate Kennedy is the author of the highly acclaimed novel *The World Beneath*, which won the People's Choice Award in the NSW Premier's Literary Awards in 2010. She is an award-winning short-story writer whose work has been published widely. Her first collection, *Dark Roots*, was shortlisted for the Steele Rudd Award in the Queensland Premier's Literary Awards and for the Australian Literature Society Gold Medal. She is also the author of a travel memoir, *Sing, and Don't Cry*, and the poetry collections *Joyflight*, *Signs of Other Fires* and *The Taste of River Water*, which won the Victorian Premier's Literary Award for Poetry in 2011. She lives on a secluded bend of the Broken River in north-east Victoria.

LIKE A HOUSE ON FIRE

—

CATE KENNEDY

SCRIBE

Melbourne • London

Scribe Publications Pty Ltd

18–20 Edward St, Brunswick, Victoria 3056, Australia
50A Kingsway Place, Sans Walk, London, EC1R 0LU, United Kingdom

First published by Scribe 2012
Reprinted 2013

Typeset in 12/17 pt Adobe Caslon Pro by the publishers
Printed and bound in Australia by Griffin Press

The paper this book is printed on is certified against the Forest
Stewardship Council® Standards. Griffin Press holds FSC chain
of custody certification SGS-COC-005088. FSC promotes
environmentally responsible, socially beneficial and economically
viable management of the world's forests.

These stories first appeared, often in slightly different forms, in the following
publications: 'Flexion', *Harvard Review* and *New Australian Stories* (Scribe, 2009);
'Ashes', *The Big Issue*; 'Laminex and Mirrors', *10 Short Stories You Must Read in 2011*
(Australia Council for the Arts, 2011); 'Tender', *The Best Australian Stories 2007*
(Black Inc., 2007) and *Wordlines* (Five Mile Press, 2010); 'Five-Dollar Family',
Overland; 'Cross-Country', *The Age* and *Summer Shorts* (Scribe, 2011); 'Sleepers',
Australian Book Review website; 'Whirlpool', *The Monthly*; 'White Spirit', *The
Best Australian Stories 2009* (Black Inc., 2009); 'Waiting', *Readings and Writings*
(Readings, 2009); 'Static', *New Australian Stories 2* (Scribe, 2010); 'Seventy-Two
Derwents', *Tales from the Tower, vol. 2: The Wicked Wood* (Allen & Unwin, 2011).

National Library of Australia
Cataloguing-in-Publication data

Kennedy, Cate.

Like a House on Fire.

9781922070067 (pbk.)

A823.4

scribepublications.com.au
scribepublications.co.uk

*For the friends who've stuck around for many years,
still talking, still laughing, still sitting around the fire,
these stories are for you, with love and gratitude.*

Contents

'In the fight between you and the world, back the world.'
—Franz Kafka

Flexion

He misjudged the bank of the dam, people said when they heard Frank Slovak had overturned his tractor onto himself. Not dead, they said, but might as well be. Caught him straight across his spine. Turning at the embankment, some loose earth, must have been looking the other way and, bang, look what happens.

His wife found him, they went on, pausing to let their listener visualise this, a nightmare they'd all had: hearing the faint throb of the tractor engine changing as it rolled, either roaring or cutting out; or else you'd be hanging out the washing, maybe, and look up to see it in the distance already on its side, metal glinting, upturned rake tines like fangs.

Everyone had imagined, sometime, making that crazed run across the paddocks, faint with whimpering dread, the air sickeningly still over your head like the eye of a storm.

Pounding through dust and weeds in that unearthly silence, steeling yourself for what you're going to find.

Yeah, his wife, they said finally, nodding. The quiet one.

Frank's wife notices the dust floating like a heat mirage as she drives up the track with the weekly shopping. She stares blankly at the silhouette on the horizon for what seems like a long time before she realises it's the huge rear wheel of the tractor she's looking at, the vehicle tipped upside down like an abandoned toy. As she runs she kicks off her slippery town shoes and feels dry furrowed earth rising and falling and crumbling under her bare feet all the way to where he's lying.

'Frank.'

Eyes rolling back to her. Collar torn off the shirt she'd just ironed the night before, and shattered glass strewn around him like crushed ice.

'Turn it off.' His voice like a bad phone connection, a robot, between locked teeth.

Shaking hand into the upside-down cabin, in and around the buckled steering wheel. Then turning the key, sliding out the familiar clinking weight of the set into her hand. Post-office-box key, car, tractor, truck, padlock for fences. They're hot from hanging in the sun. Stunned and slow, she can smell diesel dripping from the tank cap. What is he saying to her now?

'Phone.'

She instantly sees the mobile phone where she's left

it on the passenger seat of the car. It's not till she blurts this, tells him she's running back to phone the ambulance now, and sees him swallow and close his eyes instead of shouting at her, that she realises just how bad it must be. Sees too, as she pulls his shirt up to shade his eyes, that every emotion he's withheld from her for the last eighteen years, every flinch and grimace and jerk of the eyebrows and lips, is boiling and writhing across his face now. It's as if the locked strongbox inside has burst open and everything in there is rippling free and exorcised to the surface, desperately making its escape. By the time she's run home, phoned for help and returned — seven minutes there and eight-and-a-half minutes back — the spasms have stopped and he's lying there with his face as emptied as a ransacked, gaping envelope, eyes closed, doggedly sucking air in and panting it out.

You wouldn't believe it, people say when they hear the news. What caught him, what injured him most, was the bloody roll bar. The safety bar that's meant to protect you. Tell that to the Occupational Health and Safety dickheads. Some say he's crushed his pelvis, some say he's going to be a quad, but whatever it is, he's fucked now. You don't bounce back from that. And Frank Slovak, who's a glutton for work and always has been, who's got a temper like a rabid dog and a wife who wouldn't say boo, he's up in the hospital now with tubes coming out of him and they reckon the next forty-eight hours are crucial. No, it's a week now. A fortnight. He must have fractured his … what is it? The vertebrae. The nerves. The man can't feel a thing.

Frank's wife feels sympathetic eyes behind her as she wheels a trolley round the supermarket, women on the verge of saying something but thinking better of it, anxious not to be seen as nosy. After almost twenty years of near-invisibility, the accident gives her an odd kind of glamour. There are casseroles wrapped in foil left at the front door, anonymous gifts of jam and cake and soap. It's like flowers at a funeral, she thinks; a gracious gesture that comes too late, sympathy delivered once you're already dead and buried. And all for Frank, she thinks with bitterness. Frank, who'd rather cut off his own hand than be beholden to anyone, who's never put himself out for any of these people, never done them a single spontaneous good turn. Frank, who liked his privacy to the point of glowering, hostile secrecy.

The year she'd lost the baby, he'd driven her home from the hospital — the big hospital, half an hour away, so that not even the local nurses would know — and told her, looking straight ahead through the windscreen, 'We're putting this behind us.'

No jars of jam then, no lavender soap, not a word spoken or confided, until she'd felt she might go mad with the denial of it. They put it behind them, alright. They harnessed themselves to it, and dragged it like a black deadweight at their backs. They became its beasts of burden. And not a neighbour in sight, then, to drop by with a crumb of pity or a listening ear. Frank had decided that nobody was to know.

She puts the casseroles in the freezer for when she might need them more, and eats at the hospital, and as she sits in the visitors' lounge at the formica table in the air conditioning she catches herself almost revelling in the luxury of eating the first meal someone else has cooked for her in years. It's almost like being on holiday, the way they bring you a form like a menu to fill out, and come round with the trolley asking if you want tea or coffee.

There's nothing to do but wait, they tell her. Absolving her. Then Frank, greyer and gaunter by the day, contracts pneumonia. Sitting next to him in the afternoons, dozing fitfully and reading through old magazines, she listens to the laboured gurgle as he fights for breath even as he sleeps.

It must be like drowning, she thinks as she listens. Just going under, slowly losing oxygen, into blackness. Like wading into the dam; the deeper you go, the colder it gets. Something you'd almost welcome. She's shocked to acknowledge how resigned she feels to this, how it almost seems their best option, considering what prognosis the doctors gave at first. She imagines herself telling people after church: *Well, you know Frank. He wouldn't have wanted to live that way. It's for the best, really.* She thinks about serving those casseroles after the funeral, just something simple at the hall next to the church, something the auxiliary could help her organise. *I'm forty-five*, she tells herself with tentative amazement as she drives home of a night. *That's not old. Lots of women in those magazines are forty-five, and they're all getting on with life.*

At the farm someone comes without being asked and puts chains on the tractor and pulls it upright and tows it into town for repairs, and someone else, quietly and without fuss, loads the yearling lambs onto their truck and takes them off to the market for her.

Let him go, she imagines herself saying should Frank deteriorate and the hospital staff offer intubation. *It's what he would have wanted.* It startles her, this shift to being able to refer to him so readily in the past tense, a smooth, logical transition like changing gears.

But Frank beats off pneumonia, and the doctors start to say things are stabilising after the steroids and there might yet be a partial recovery after all, some limited movement, it's hard to say, and she sits composing her face into relief and optimism while inside, truth be known, she feels cheated. Cheated as she watches Frank lifting a spoon to his face, scowling with a kind of ferocious, vindictive resolve, like he's going to hit someone. Relearning it all like an automaton, determined to heave himself back.

'I'm not going to be a burden on anyone, is that clear?' he mutters to her when the physios finally leave them alone for the afternoon. And knocks her hand away, as she goes to wipe some gravy off his chin.

That's Frank all over. Can't hold a fork, but can still find a way to smack her out of the way.

It's easier to nod and agree, to pretend to take his advice about what she should be doing about the farm work. Nearly two months pass and she expects any day that one of these rehabilitation workers is going to read him the riot act and tell him he's mad to think he's going to return to the farm, and this anticipation, this certainty, fills her with suppressed, patient hope.

Maybe he'll survive, maybe he's not going to be in a hospital the rest of his life, but the argument's over; they'll have to move now, in any case, into town. A little unit or bungalow. Something new, with no steps anywhere because of the wheelchair. She'll be able to walk into town every day to shop for whatever she needs, and there'll probably have to be home help, which would give her breaks; it would be taken as read that she'd need breaks — they even give her the pamphlets explaining what she'll be entitled to.

She might even get a carer's pension, on top of the insurance and what they get for the farm. A new car, maybe, with one of those hoists.

This daydreaming is halted the day Frank claws himself up onto the machinery at the physiotherapy unit, growling like an animal and swearing a blue streak, his eyes popping with the strain, and as she watches in incredulous despair his left leg jerks itself out and wavers hesitantly above the rubber flooring, like someone learning to dance.

And while the physio shakes her head in admiration, the doctors confer over his X-rays, making up new explanations for her, saying, 'He's recovered a great deal more function than we first anticipated, it's excellent news,' and all the time she's standing there nodding like a doll, hating him so much she can't trust herself to open her mouth.

That afternoon when she goes home the plumber is there, the same plumber who'd quoted her something impossible last year when she'd asked how much it would cost to bring the toilet inside. Only now he and his assistant are installing a brand-new modular shower unit and sink with chrome railings, telling her it's no trouble, anything for old Frank, we'll have this finished in no time and get out of your way, Mrs Slovak.

'You tell him hello from Pete and Hardo,' the plumber says as he leaves, 'and tell him Bob Wilkes says he'll get his hay baled for him and into the shed no trouble this week, so don't worry about a thing.'

And once again, trying to show brightness and gratitude while inside her, choking rage burns like a grassfire, like gasoline.

Because now any fool can see how it's going to be. Frank unable to sit at the desk, standing over her telling her how to do the books, ordering her round and snapping at her. In the ute beside her as she drives, sighing with contempt every time she crunches the gears, unable even to get out and open the gates for her, Frank hovering over her entire working day, badgering her and criticising her and depending on her for everything. And her, running the gauntlet outside church and in town, having to dutifully tell everyone how lucky they'd been.

Limited mobility is actually going to suit Frank, she thinks; he's been minimising all his movements for years, barely turning his head to her when she speaks, sitting there stonily in the kitchen, immoveable as a mountain. Unbending. So now, with his back fused like he's got a poker rammed down it, on one or two sticks or a walking frame, the doctors say, depending on how well his pelvis adapts, it will be Frank needing her to pull his legs sideways out of the bed and haul him into a sitting position and run for cushions and there won't need to be home help for that; they won't qualify. The community worker will come to assess them and see how well she can cope, and Frank will tell them he doesn't need help, thanks all the same, he's got all the help he needs. It's marvellous, people will say to her after church, the way God works.

'This your doing?' is all he says when he sees the bathroom. 'Couldn't wait to go behind my back?'

'Nothing to do with me. Pete Nichol did it.'

He shoots her a look. 'What — just turned up and did it? That'll be the day.'

Heaves himself forward on his frame to get a better look at the fitting around the sink, grunts dismissively when he can't find anything wrong with it.

'Better get ready to remortgage the place, then, for when his bill comes. Common knowledge the man charges like a wounded bull.'

'He said not to worry about it.' She tries not to make her voice sound too enthused, to give him less ammunition. It's a skill, doing that.

'What's through there?' He can't jerk his head now, she notices. Just his eyes.

'The new toilet.'

'You're bloody joking.' He shoulders past her and inches over there, crablike. He looks around the door suspiciously then grunts again.

'Well, he's left me in the shit now with council, that's all I can say. They'll be straight onto me about having to pay for an easement. They don't miss a trick, those bastards.'

'Frank, he said he sorted the easement. Left me the permit and papers and everything. They're in on the desk.'

He pivots again, swearing as the wheels on the frame bang into the bath, to find her standing in front of him, waiting for his reaction. It would kill him, she thinks, to show pleasure or relief or excitement. Her loathing is such a pure thing she experiences a secret visceral pleasure to watch him cornered like this, tormented by something as incomprehensible and enraging as kindness.

'So who came and dug the trench?' he snaps accusingly.

'That contractor he uses, Ian Harding, is it?'

'How much did he charge?'

'I'm telling you, they said not to worry about it.'

He actually grimaces with discomfort, muttering at her to get out of his way as he shuffles past. Bangs out the back door and down the brand-new ramp that someone from Rotary came and fitted last week, replacing the back step that had been broken for almost eleven years. At the end of the backyard, in sight of the hay shed, he stops short and stares at his neatly slashed paddocks and stacked bales. It's then she sees what his limited mobility is costing him now; how his neck and head are forced to stay erect while his shoulders sag at a stiff helpless angle, hands clinging to the brakes of his walking frame, the whole of him fighting against the suppressed tremors that threaten to shake him free of it.

'Bob Wilkes did it,' she calls, but he doesn't turn or respond. She imagines him giving up and toppling, curled there on the ground. She's never seen him curled up, not even when she sat there with him in the dirt, waiting for the ambulance. He'd stayed in control then too, sprawled there licking his lips every now and again, his eyes losing focus with something like bewilderment as he stared up into the blue, something almost innocent.

'You just have to do this till I get the hang of it,' he mutters as she helps him manoeuvre into the shower.

She ignores him, just goes on explaining. 'Now you

lower yourself onto the seat using the handrails and back out your walker because you're not supposed to get it wet.'

'Right. I'll be right now.'

'Well, I'll just stay and turn on the taps. See, they're low — they put them there specially.'

'Be easier if I could stand up. Reach the bloody soap myself then.'

'I'll look out for one of those soap-on-a-rope things.'

God, the flesh is hanging off him. His knuckles are white and waxy as they cling to the handles; he's as scared and frail as an old, old man. Scared to turn his head or take one hand off the rail. One misstep away from a nursing home. His hair needs a cut and she decides she'll do it later at the kitchen table.

'That's better,' he says as she adjusts the hot tap.

And she can hear that he's about to say thank you, then stops and swallows. Even without the thanks, though, she thinks it's probably the longest conversation they've had for months.

'Now you need to put the brake locks on this every time you pull up, understand? Don't forget — up with the handrails, step onto the rubber mat, both hands on the walker handles then release the brake.'

'I'm not stupid,' he mutters, but his eyes are following her every move, the pupils dilated.

She gets him dressed and into the kitchen, cuts his hair and shaves him. One of the casseroles, defrosted, with rice — he can manage that. Then she tears a page off the pad and lays it down in front of him, places the cordless phone handset next to him.

'What's this?'

'Phone numbers. You've got some calls to make.' She feels a surge of courage as she says it, there on the other side of the table. She taps the list. 'People to ring and thank, now you're home.'

'Don't bloody start that nonsense. I didn't ask for any of those do-gooders to come around.'

'Frank,' she says. 'I'm not arguing with you, I'm telling you. If you ever want another favour done, and believe me you're going to be calling in a few, ring and let people know how much you appreciate what they've done for you.'

'Or what?' He looks strange, fighting to maintain an attitude of derisive scorn as he sits there in pyjamas, his hair neatly combed and the muscles wasted on him after all these months on his back.

'What do you reckon?' she says, exasperated. 'We go under. We sell up.'

And when he looks at her with familiar, narrow contempt, she picks up the hand mirror, lying there next to the scissors on the table, and a steady exhilaration pumps through her as she deliberately angles it to face him.

'Take a good look,' she says, 'and get on that phone.'

In bed, already planning in her mind the tasks of the next day, she listens to the fan ticking over their heads and feels the forgotten, heavy presence of him lying beside her. She thinks about the physiotherapist at the hospital, lifting Frank's legs and folding them against his body, turning him on his side and gently bending his arms from shoulder to hip. Flexion, she'd called it. Exercises to flex the muscles and keep the memory of limber movement alive in the body, to stop those ligaments and tendons tightening and atrophying away.

'Just like this, Mr Slovak,' she'd said, that calm and cheerful young woman. 'You can do these yourself, just keep at it,' and she'd taken Frank's hand and made his arm describe a slow circle, then flexed the elbow to make it touch his chest. Down and back again, over and over; a gesture like a woodenly acted entreaty. 'Do you want me to leave you this page of instructions on these movements, to jog your memory?'

Frank, submitting hatchet-faced to the procedure, had given his head one slow, stiff shake. 'If I need a set of instructions to remember that,' he said tightly, 'you may as well carry me out in a box right now.'

The girl had just laughed indulgently at him, she remembers now. She must send those staff members a card and a present, thank them all for their forbearance.

She hears Frank exhale, then silence before a ragged, hiccuping intake of breath. She glances over and makes out the shape of him in the moony dimness, flat on his back and still as a tree, arms at his sides like a soldier at attention, and crying soundlessly, eyes screwed shut and face contorted into a mask. His mouth is a black hole of terror. Glinting tears leak into the furrows of discontent etched around his eyes and nose, pour down to wet his freshly barbered hair. She's never seen this, and it's mortifying. They'd warned her about acute pain; she wonders about getting up and giving him some tablets, but she's so shocked all she can do is turn her head back to look up at the ceiling and spare him the shame of her scrutiny. They lie rigidly side by side.

'When you stood up to run home and call the ambulance,' he says, 'I thought, well, now I've got ten minutes. Now would be the good time to die, while you weren't there. That's what I could give you.'

Lying there, she has a sense of how it is, suddenly: willing your limbs to move but being unable to lift them. The terrible treasonous distance between them that must be traversed, the numbed heaviness of her arm.

But she finally reaches over and takes his hand. It doesn't even feel like his anymore; the working calluses vanished into soft smoothness like a beach after a stormy receding tide. She wouldn't recognise this hand now, especially not the way the fingers grip hers. *Squeeze my hand*, the physio had said. *That's good, Mr Slovak.*

She lies there feeling the pulse in her husband's pitifully thin wrist under her little finger. She understands better than anyone, she thinks, the painful stretch of sinew, the crack of dislocation. Remembers herself running back over the paddocks, flying barefoot over stones and earth, looking down distractedly in the ambulance later to notice the dried blood on her feet. How fast she'd run, and how much faster she'd run back. Now, in the dark bed, she raises her arm with Frank's and gently flexes both their elbows together. She places his hand wordlessly, determinedly, over his heart, and holds it there.

Ashes

By the time they stop at a cafe for the obligatory morning tea, Chris is already feeling his staunch goodwill leaking away. Enervating, to be in her presence like this. Despite all his resolve to stay pleasant and attentive, today of all days, something has nevertheless turned a tap on inside him and his energy is draining away. Later he'll feel the same guilt as ever, but right now, sitting with a coffee listening to his mother complaining about the fake whipped cream on her scones, he feels all that evaporating. Ten-thirty in the morning, and he's already itching with it.

He just has to keep his mood on the good side of surliness. And surely even his mother would forgive him a touch of melancholia today, considering the occasion. He sees her fastidiously scrape the cream off the scones, making sure the waitress is watching, and pile it distastefully on the side of her plate. She's dressed up today, hair done, lipstick matching the red blazer. Black shoes with heels. He'd told her to dress in something easy to walk in, because he remembered there was some walking involved, but it was like talking to a brick wall. She'd be able to stop now on the walk, grimace and suffer. Talk about her blisters for weeks afterwards with her book club women.

He thinks of them in formidable capitals: the Book Club Women. Women perennially sitting around modular lounge suites, criticising someone's book. His mother keeps photos of the grandchildren of the Book Club Women on her own fridge, like a silently accusing rebuke every time he walks past.

'Dear little Justin started his swimming lessons last week,' she'll say, smiling out at something through the screen door.

'Sorry? I'm not sure I know who Justin is.'

She'll tut impatiently. 'Oh, of course you do, Christopher. Sandra's grandson.'

He'll be struggling to place Sandra while she continues on another tangent.

'Well, Caroline's really in a tizz over this wedding. She wants Pam to go up there to help her, all the way to Brisbane. She'll have to change her tune pretty quick smart once she marries that James fellow. Can't be calling on her mother to be at her beck and call all the time.' She'll hesitate, as if reluctant to betray something confided in her, although Chris has heard this postscript every time Caroline is mentioned. 'You know they had to get counselling when she was a teenager once. Ran right off the rails.'

Chris will nod, follow her gaze out through the glass door to the leaf-littered garden. She's talking about hiring a gardener now, to deal with it. His father's rakes and brooms stand stiffly to attention beside the locked shed.

Since his father died, Chris keeps coming across small reminders everywhere, set like mousetraps ready to snap, like little buried landmines. Today, for instance, they're in his father's car, which his mother says she can't bear to sell. It smells so characteristically, still, of shoe polish and peppermints, and in the back seat lies the woollen tartan scarf his father had worn for years. Each detail had assailed Chris as he'd opened the door, reaching over to stow the box in its calico bag on the back seat.

'Here, here,' his mother had remonstrated. 'At my feet.'

Where else? he'd thought sourly, finding the right key for the ignition, as the lifetime habit of keeping his responses to himself closed his mouth in a firm and well-worn line. A line that suggested nothing, broached nothing, gave nothing away.

'Five dollars for those scones,' his mother says as they walk out of the cafe. 'Honestly.' The Book Club Women, Chris thinks, will hear about this. Back at the car, as he waits for her to catch up, he fumbles for the self-locking device on the key ring, finding the one for the boot so he can take the bag out again. His mother had insisted they park the car in view of the cafe so she could watch it for potential theft. 'It's bad enough leaving him there in the boot like that,' she'd said, digging in her bag for a tissue, 'without risking someone stealing him.'

'Take the bag in with us, then,' he'd suggested.

She'd glared, aghast. 'I couldn't possibly.'

He's noticed she can hardly bring herself to touch the box. It's like some huge supernatural power emanates from it.

When they'd gone to get it from the crematorium, she'd stood silent, locking her hands tightly together, leaving it to him to pick it up, sign for it, and ask for a carry bag. It wasn't until they were outside that she'd burst out with a tirade about how disrespectful it was not to provide families with an urn, or something appropriate. A box, she'd hissed all the way home, fuelled by the outrage of it, nothing but a box. He expected tears, but there were none. Instead, once home, she'd led the way to her antique cabinet, unlocked it, and stood back while he pushed the box inside, in there among the gold-leaf dinner service he remembered so well from his parents' dinner parties when he was a child. As he'd straightened up after putting his father's ashes inside the cabinet, he longed so much to be with Scott that it almost hurt.

It hit him still sometimes when he least expected it, even after three years: moments when he missed him with an intensity almost like an electric shock; something searing that flashed and left a lingering ache. Scott would have known exactly what to do — pour them both a whisky, probably, and then sit him on the verandah talking till they'd killed the whole bottle. Chris wouldn't have been standing here now, either, feeling useless and tongue-tied, embarrassed by the floundering pause between his mother and himself, like two strangers observing someone else's ritual. Scott would have known how to give the moment some ceremony.

He stands beside the car dangling the bag, waiting for her as she pauses by a craft shop and browses through things outside in a rustic barrow. Chris can see what's piled there — miniature teddies, lavender sachets, fabrics. She has a wardrobe full of unfinished craft projects at home, although, thank Christ, he suspects she's finally given up and stopped knitting baby clothes. Totally absorbed, she picks up a bag of bath salts and examines it with all the time in the world.

'Your mother could shop in a service station,' his father used to say, poker-faced. He'd wait outside countless shops for her in an attitude just like Chris's now, leaning resignedly against the car. She'll want something to commemorate the trip, Chris knows, a souvenir she can store on a shelf and refer to bravely, and sure enough she gets back in the car with a paper bag.

'Lovely silver frame,' she murmurs. 'Half price. There were a few of them too. I wonder if I should have got one for Pam.' She sighs, comforted by her purchase, the slight of the fake cream forgotten.

Chris is looking for the turn-off. He thinks he'll know it when he sees it, although he hasn't been up here for twenty-five years. Then another twenty kilometres or so to get to the lake. As far as he can remember there's a little jetty there, past the campsites — a good spot to stand and do it, rather than the muddy shore. He's got the digital camera all charged up.

His father's car has some kind of cruise-control check that beeps at him every time he inadvertently goes above the set limit, and he keeps jumping when he hears it, feeling a ludicrous start of guilt. The late-morning heat in the car is making the familiar smell of his father even stronger. When was the last time he'd stood close enough to his father to inhale the real thing? Not at the hospital; nothing there but the smell of antiseptic and drugs. He punches a CD into the player and another little memory-bomb goes off in the back of his head — it's the Three Tenors, the CD he bought for his parents two Christmases ago. That would have been the last time: a fraternal, quick arm-squeeze and back-slap, both glad to have it over.

There's a headache starting behind his eyes. He can feel what's coming: his mother wants to talk, and he must pay attention to divert her in time from dangerous territory.

'People said the service was so lovely and dignified,' she begins. 'Graham and Laura were asking me whether I was going to have a memorial plaque for your father at the crematorium gardens. Well, I went out with Neil and Shirley to have a look, because that's what Elaine did when John died, but Laura told me it cost her thousands. And they don't even inter the ashes, just scatter them. It's all just garden beds, you know; it's not as if there's even an actual plot.'

Chris waits for the next bit, about the lake. He can't help it, this roiling, sneering intolerance. She's grieving, he knows; vulnerable, needing contact, prone to these banal litanies of repetition, but he just can't help it. He clenches his jaw.

'I told them we'd just be going to the lake, just the family. It's better to do something that's meaningful to Chris and me, that Alan would have wanted, I said.'

She pauses. Here it comes.

'Those trips to the lake with you were very special to your father, Chris.'

He grunts his assent. He can't bring himself to answer, in case he gets some detail wrong.

'I told Shirley, that's where he'd rather be laid to rest, in the place where he shared such precious times with his son. He had lots of happy memories of all those fishing trips.'

All those fishing trips. They'd been twice. Once at the Easter break, and once for the first week of the September school holidays. After that his father had given up. Both trips are still etched vividly in Chris's mind, like so many of the powerless indignities of childhood. His father's attempts at blokey conversation puttering out like the dinghy's outboard, sighing as it gave up the ghost in a bank of weeds, Chris feeling sick with the stink of petrol, his father's barely concealed disgust when he unwisely asked if he could take his book out on the boat with them the next day. At night they'd sit in front of their tent, waiting for it to get dark, both of them without a thing to say beyond their usual wary exchanges. His father's forced cheeriness slowly evaporating into his usual taciturnity as he got tired of trying. Chris coughing in the acrid smoke. Trying not to move too much in the stuffy sleeping bag at night. Then the packing of the car on the last day, the esky empty and leaking melted ice, and his obscure sense that he'd failed some test.

'I don't know what's bloody wrong with you,' his father had muttered as they drove back down this very road after the second trip. Chris had wanted to say something, some retort that would salvage some pride, but his mouth had felt dry, scorched somehow. He was eleven … no, twelve, and starting to get a glimmer that there was something deeply dissatisfying about him, something that baffled his father and pinned a strained, mortified smile on his mother's face when they had visitors. Neither of them, not his father nor his mother, had any idea how to name what the thing was. He'd just look up sometimes and catch it in their faces; something like fear. It wasn't till uni that what was *wrong with him* had hit him square in the face at last, with a flash of realisation that was so clichéd it was almost comical. He'd expected commiseration when he'd related the father–son trips to Scott one time, but Scott had collapsed with mirth instead.

'Jesus, that's priceless,' he'd said. 'What a hoot.'

'It wasn't a hoot, it was bloody excruciating. Like a punishment.'

'Lighten up. You're not the first gay man whose parents didn't understand him.'

'Don't tell me, it's all part of the journey,' Chris had said.

Scott had waved his bitterness off, like it wasn't worth rising to the bait for. 'Well, yeah,' he'd said mildly. 'It is. No point blaming them. Move on. That's what I say.'

It was Scott who'd moved on, though. Chris had been going to introduce him to his parents, he just had to wait for the right moment, he'd told Scott in increasing tones of self-recrimination. It wasn't as if he was ashamed of him, God no. But he'd gone anyway.

Chris thinks now of the last time he'd seen his father, in the hospital after the surgery. It must have been the morphine that had removed the usual armour of avoidance.

'Your mother gone down to check out the gift shop, has she?' his father had muttered, the words slurring. The corner of his mouth lifted in a small wry smile.

Chris swallowed and squeezed the arm lying slackly on the white sheets. 'She has, yes. Or down for a coffee.' He smiled back, too hard.

'Your mother,' said his father. There was a pause, like the frequency had gone off the airwaves momentarily, or he was sifting through a limited selection of words. 'Your mother's always been proud of you, Chris. In her own way.'

Chris's hand stayed on the arm, patting now. *Don't tell me it's going to be now*, he thought with disbelief. *Don't you dare address this now, when it's all too late.*

His father licked his lips. 'You obviously ... you've got to live the way you see fit.' He was whispering. Every word like a pulling stitch as he panted slightly, eyes shut tight against the possibility of looking his son in the eye. 'But there's no need to ... well ... throw it in her face. It would kill her.'

Spending his last hours worrying about her. It had killed him, not her. He'd taken that tiny admission, heavy and impervious as a lead sinker, and clung on to its icy weight all the way down to the depths. A secretive man, Chris thinks now. The irony is not lost on him that he has that insight because he has become one himself.

More than ever since the funeral, his mother has embellished past events to give them a patina of something richer and happier. Every time he visits, it seems, they're embroidered more until the truth as he remembers it is buried under stiff layers of decorative restitching. When his father was alive, she'd railed for years at his morose passivity, heaped bitterness and blame upon him for keeping her locked in a dull and predictable life. Chris recalls the way she used to speak to him, like he was a slow-witted employee; her eye-rolling, histrionic exasperation at the slightest mishap. All that is gone now.

Instead she reminisces with a sweet, sad smile about his patience, his bumbling good intentions. 'What a shame you never thought to take photos on those trips,' she says fretfully. 'Your father would have loved a record of them.'

Chris jumps again as the car beeps at him accusingly, and he shifts against the sheepskin seat-cover. His mother sighs, looks out the window. 'He loved coming up here with you,' she repeats, half to herself.

It's nauseating, this revisionism; it infuriates him. This, he thinks savagely, this is the best she can summon: the two of them travelling alone to enact a ceremony in the presence of no lifelong friends, no neighbours who care enough, no extended family, in a place whose symbolism is wholly an invention. *This is the reality*, he imagines saying to her, *just you and me, your 35-year-old son who you cast as the perennial bachelor, this pitiful pilgrimage I can't wait to be finished with.* The words rage in his head, smoking like acid in behind his clamped mouth. He sees the sign to the lake come up over a crest, and the car's computer beeps at him again, like his father nudging him in the ribs, wordless and critical, as Chris snaps on the indicator.

Of late, his mother's started inviting him over to dinner during the week, and he's been realising with a sinking feeling that she's delaying serving the meal until later and later in the evening.

'Just stay and watch the news with me,' she'll say then, topping up his wine after they've washed the dishes, and Chris watches it, itching to be gone. 'You could always stay the night, if it's too late to drive home,' will be her next gambit, and he can't stand the studied casualness in her voice, the pretence of spontaneity. 'Your bed's all made up. You could just shower and go straight to work in the morning.'

'Mum, I've really got to go …'

'Grab a towel and there's plenty of clean shirts up there, just have a shower and drive to work straight from here,' she repeats, and behind the warmth in her tone he can hear the steely undercurrent she'd used on him as a child to make him do as he was told.

He knows where all these invitations are leading, and already feels exhausted with the thought of what hopes will have to be quashed before much longer.

Soon she won't camouflage her disappointment so well, and then she'll raise the stakes. 'I don't understand why you can't just *stay*,' she'll say petulantly. 'I know you'll think I'm stupid but I feel nervous here alone in the house at night.' She will pause, he is certain, and then add, 'And it's not as if you've got a wife and children at home waiting, is it?'

The whole campsite looks different — enlarged with signposted nature trails, composting toilets, designated fireplaces. Chris thinks of gathering wood all those years ago, his father's lecture, as they walked, about snakes and bushfires. The way he'd taken a trowel he'd brought along specially and dug a shallow rectangular hole for their campfire, and laid the sticks out in a grid.

His mother puffs a little as she walks up the sandy track from the car park, and Chris consciously slows his walk down. The thought that she might want him to say something, some kind of spoken farewell on the jetty, fills him with a queasy panic. It was bad enough doing the eulogy at the funeral, then he'd amazed himself by breaking down afterwards, while he was talking to the minister at the reception. The other man had stood patiently, holding a cup of tea, as Chris snuffled into a handkerchief, fighting to regain his composure. How could he even begin to tell this stranger what he was really grieving for? He'd taken a breath before realising he couldn't even articulate what it was himself. Just the strain of the day, he thinks now. Keeping it all together.

They reach the jetty that he remembers, and his mother makes a little exclamation of relief.

'Oh, this is lovely,' she says. Her voice is trembling. 'I don't want to say anything, Chris. I just want to do it. But it's so hard. I should have opened the box and saved some, to keep for myself.'

He hurriedly feels in his pocket for some kind of

container. 'We'll pop some ashes in the camera bag,' he says. 'Then you can take some home with you and scatter them under the roses, maybe.' He's desperate for a quick solution, to stop her dissolving into maudlin helplessness; he's the one with the resolve. 'The camera bag,' he repeats with an indulgent chuckle. 'Imagine what he would have had to say about that!'

He's rewarded with a wan smile. 'Better than a matchbox. Remember how he always hated me smoking, till I finally gave up?'

Chris walks to the end of the jetty and extracts the box from the bag, crouching on the weathered boards to open it. Inside, there is a square polystyrene tub, securely sealed with tape. He picks at it.

'Here,' says his mother, surprising him. She hands him a pair of nail scissors and he holds their sharp coolness in his hand for a moment, pausing.

In a minute, he thinks, stalling. *Not just yet.*

'Lovely we've got the place to ourselves,' she murmurs. 'I'd hate there to be anyone else here. Lovely to have the privacy.'

Chris glances up, out across the glittering water, wishing he'd worn his sunglasses. He has a sudden clear memory of his father, sitting in the dinghy, both their rods swinging without bait and the fishing forgotten. His father had sat squinting out at the glassy still surface of water all around them, disconcertingly unfamiliar in his cotton sports shirt and towelling hat.

'Don't reckon we'll catch anything, do you?' he'd said.

Chris remembers shaking his head.

'Not that it matters, though. Just good to be out here, isn't it?'

It's funny, he'd forgotten that moment until now. His father's hopeful smile.

Chris rises and takes a photo of his mother standing on the end of the jetty in her red blazer.

'Pick up the box,' he calls, peering into the viewfinder. She hesitates, then lifts it, holding it close against her chest, square and plain against her flowered scarf. Chris imagines her looking in the mirror that morning, trying the scarf on, lifting her chin in that way she has, every small decision an aching effort. He wishes he'd told her she looked nice, when he'd arrived at her door. Her expression as she faces the camera, obedient and tremulous and trying not to blink, makes his throat feel tight; there is a stinging behind his eyes. He takes the photo, then hurries back over to her and slices open the tape. He lifts the lid off and sees conflicting emotion on her face as she takes one panicked glance into the tub, her jaw clenching as she jerks her eyes away, over at the water again.

'You,' is all she says.

No possibility that Chris might be permitted to feel the same violent shirking resistance, no likelihood that he will just be able to stand and upend the box and shake its contents into the water without touching them. No. Now that push has come to shove, it's going to be him.

A handful of coarse sand is what it feels like. That's all. He pinches some of it between his fingers and lets it sift down into the water. He remembers that they had both crouched here with saucepans and cleaned them with river sand, then filled them to pour onto the grey ashy coals of the campfire, the day they'd broken camp to go home. His father had trodden the coals down, crushing them neatly, scattered some soil over the top just like Chris is scattering the contents of the box now over the water. Small handfuls. That smell of wet ash, and the cicadas beating like the ticking of a clock, and his father giving the site one last glance around and saying, 'Great spot anyway, don't you reckon, Chris?'

Why hadn't he answered with enthusiastic assent? What would it have cost him to give his father that, instead of a shrug, just for the small mean pleasure of feeling his father turn away, defeated? He scoops up another handful and spills it into the water. A drift of grey and white particles swirls on the surface and disperses. He can't believe this is all that's left, this dust and grit, pounded down from something as hard and unyielding as bone.

'Goodbye, Alan,' he hears his mother whisper, over and over, until the box is empty.

The two of them stand there as she mechanically folds and refolds the calico bag, weeping, shifting in her uncomfortable shoes.

Why hadn't he answered? He stoops and rinses his

hands in the shallows, sick with the memory, the waste of it. The heat of the afternoon makes a chorus of cicadas gust up; still that throbbing tick like a heartbeat, measuring out the uncounted hours.

'You OK to go?' he says finally.

By the time they are back at the car, she's recovered herself sufficiently to wonder if they might get back to that gift shop before closing time, so she can buy those other frames. They can be gifts, she tells him, her animation returning with this new sense of purpose, for the ladies in the book club, to thank them for all the support they've given her.

Chris thinks they can probably get back there by 4.30. As he nods and agrees what a nice gesture it would be, he sees a small smear of ash on the lapel of her jacket, and absently, tenderly, without interrupting her, he brushes it off.

Laminex and Mirrors

Laminex and mirrors, that's me. Or at least that's meant to be me. That's my own particular jurisdiction, I discover when I arrive at dawn on my first day at the hospital and am solemnly handed gloves, a cloth and a spray bottle.

The other cleaners have got their pace down to an art, and it is the pace of the patients themselves, shuffling along the hospital corridors with their drips and tangled tubing; the slow, measured perambulation of those with an endless, unvarying stretch in front of them.

The cleaners spin out their morning's tasks, glazed and unhurried. I don't get this at first. Not quite eighteen and fresh out of school, I'm saving money to go to London and I'm eager-beavering my way through my allotted duties on this holiday job, intent on making a good impression.

Marie, the head cleaner, is annoyed with me

when I finish early on that first day and seek her out, conscientiously, for another job. I surprise her in the linen cupboard, feet up on a chair and the daily paper opened to the births and deaths.

'I've finished!' I announce as she looks up, startled and sprung.

'Have you now?' She smiles thinly, a cup of tea and two biscuits balanced on her palm. 'Well, Dot's on bedding today and Noeleen's doing floors. So you can ... clean out the ash bins.'

At the grand entrance to the hospital stand two tall black bins for cigarette butts and other detritus abandoned by hurrying visitors, things smoked and gulped and discarded as nervous relatives pace outside. Inside each can is a toxic soup of ash, butts, coffee and polystyrene. I tip each bin into the industrial skip, groping for the high-pressure hose, the smell of them making me turn away and retch until tears come to my eyes. The smell will stay hanging on me all day, burned and stale; Marie's revenge on me, I realise belatedly, for working too briskly.

We break at 7 a.m. to sit in the kitchen and drink tea from thick cups while the catering staff stands at the huge industrial benches stirring gigantic tureens of custard and tomato soup. Dot tries to sell us mail-order cosmetics and cleaning products. She's nervy and keen to please, cheerfully volunteering for the unpleasant jobs. I've never met anyone like Dot, whose hair is backcombed into an actual beehive and who blinks hard with watery-eyed nervousness when anyone addresses her directly. While we're restocking the paper towels in the toilets, though, she tells me the best-value toilet paper to buy, the one that's rolled more tightly than the others, so you get more. It's criminal, in Dot's opinion, what those toilet-roll companies are allowed to get away with.

'Well, thanks for the tip,' I say as she heads off along the corridors with a wheelie bucket and mop, ready to attack the expanse of cafeteria floor. Lysol is still stinging my nostrils from the emptied ash bins, now sitting pristine back at the entrance, and I have already made a lifetime vow this morning to never smoke.

One of the patients calls me back when I've finished cleaning his room. An old bloke, ex-Army.

'You look like a lovely girl,' he rasps, grabbing for my wrist. 'There's a few dollars in my bedside table there, how would you like to do an old man a favour and go down to the kiosk and buy me a packet of smokes?' He names the brand, his gaze upon me steady and desperately hopeful.

Under no circumstances, the matron has already told me, her lips stiff with disapproval, am I to comply with this request. The man's dying, his lungs already clagged with tar, it's unbelievable. He tries it on with everyone.

I smile apologetically at him. 'Sorry, Mr Moreton.'

'Matron's got to you, has she?'

'Sorry, but yes.'

'Dunno what's gunna kill me first,' he mutters.

I give his breakfast tray an ineffectual rub. He hasn't touched his poached egg, and I can't blame him — it's sitting there like the eye of a giant squid. Mr Moreton has an oxygen mask, but tells me he hates using it.

'Feel like that thing's choking me,' he says. 'Like in the war.' Constrained in his bed, he lies with his fingers constantly rubbing each other, missing the smokes.

Mr Moreton's never asleep, even at 5.30 a.m. when I clock on.

'How are you today?' I say to him each morning as I spray and wipe his perfectly clean mirror.

'No good,' he whispers, his frail pigeon chest sucking the air in. 'You don't feel like just bringing me in one ciggy, do ya, and wheeling me out there onto the verandah?'

He jerks his head towards the courtyard visible from his double-glazed window; a Rotary-sponsored rose garden manicured to within an inch of its life.

'I'm sorry, Mr Moreton. Matron would kill me.'

'Yeah, I know the feeling.'

I linger a few minutes, and we chat, his wheezing laugh threatening, always, to turn into a coughing fit.

'I know you're a friendly girl,' says one of the nurses in low, embarrassed tones when she stops me in the corridor a few minutes later, 'but it's best not to fraternise too much with the patients. If you're a cleaner, I mean.'

'Right,' I say. 'Sorry.'

'Just do your work.'

'Sorry, I will.'

I trudge, my face burning, down towards the corridor of elective surgeries. It's OK, I tell myself. At the end of the summer holidays I will have saved enough for three months in Europe, where I will walk the streets of Paris and London, absorbing culture and life and fraternising with whoever I like. Down in electives, bed after bed is filled with miserable girls with two black eyes and post-rhinoplasty noses swathed in bandages.

'My parents gave me this for me twenty-first,' one honks dolefully as I spray her mirror. 'If I'd have known it was going to hurt like this I wouldn't have had it done. Just look at my eyes.'

She gazes over my shoulder into the mirror with the fretful, restless scrutiny that has caused all this fault-finding in the first place. You can't tell if she's pretty or not because of the swelling and bruising, and the black rim of blood around each nostril. She sighs and climbs back into bed with her magazine. The room smells of nail polish and expensive bunches of flowers. Soon the hospital, I'm told, is going private, and every wing will be like this one, with glistening white ensuite bathrooms and upmarket floral bedspreads in every room.

Down in the oldest public wing there is an ancient bathroom slated for demolition, with three huge enamel baths inside. Rust-coloured marks streak the surface under the chrome taps, where millions of leaks have dripped year after year after year, and whenever I glance in and see them I think of sick patients in the old days, lying awake in their beds listening to that nocturnal dripping like a relentless echoing clock, marking their time left.

Each idle post-op girl, surrounded by hothouse flowers, watches me with the same bored, incurious gaze as I move about their rooms, spraying and wiping. I pump mist over the immaculate mirrors, catching sight of my own reflection there — my unreconstructed nose and studiously neutral face. Like these girls, I'm filling in my own allotment of time here, except that when I leave, it'll be to buy that plane ticket to London, and be gone. My hand holding the yellow cloth rises and falls, cleaning pointlessly, searching for a splash of toothpaste or cup ring mark on the laminex's spotless, glossy surface.

'You know what I've found,' Dot says as she passes me in the corridor, pointing to my blue spray bottle. 'Don't even use those commercial cleaners. Metho and newspaper, that's the best thing for cleaning windows and mirrors.'

'But, Dot,' I say, 'don't you sell all those cleaning products?'

'I do,' she concedes. 'But it's the cosmetics I believe in.'

That morning at tea-break, she slides a catalogue and an order form in front of me as if it's already a done deal. 'And have a look at the jewellery,' she whispers, tapping the catalogue eagerly. 'So reasonable.'

Marie puts down her teacup and gives me a shrewd

look. 'Do you think you're ready for more responsibility?' she asks.

I look up from the page of friendship rings. 'Well, I guess so. Yes.'

'Can you operate a floor polisher?'

I've seen the ones she means — the massive hydraulic polishers in the storeroom.

'What about Noeleen?'

'Her back's giving her trouble.'

'OK, I'll give it a go.'

Dot's looking at me hard, blinking. 'If you could just fill in what you want before you go, I can get the order off in time for the Christmas discount,' she says.

I am caught in the high-beam of her earnest gratitude, the undiluted optimism of her pale blue eyes. Dot's husband, Len, can't take her home business seriously, she's told me. He doesn't think she's got what it takes to sell enough jewellery and make-up to be eligible for a Christmas bonus gift.

I've met Len. He often joins us at morning tea on his way home from the night shift at the printing works, and his coiffed ducktail matches his wife's beehive in a way that makes me wonder where they met and in what year.

'The corridor down to surgery,' Marie says. She hands me a bundle of steel wool. 'For all the wheel marks,' she adds.

The hand controls of the hydraulic polisher judder and jar out of my grasp as the spinning discs hit the floor and grab. It takes off like a bronco.

'Use your hips, girl!' says Noeleen, as I let it go in a panic and we lean against the wall, weak with laughter.

She's right. When I nudge the polisher along with my hips and keep my arms held tight at my sides, I can get the thing under control. I waltz the linoleum corridors in big sweeping arcs, walking backwards, making everything shine, singing top-forty songs to myself. There's the good clean smell of metho where Dot's polished the glass doors, and the deafening whine of the machine like white noise, erasing the tedium.

Then I get down on my hands and knees and scrub with the steel wool at the black rubber streaks left by the wheels of the surgical trolleys. Sometimes, even as I'm scrubbing, a new trolley bangs through the doors, and I crawl out of the way to give it room to lay a new purposeful trail of black streaks for me.

Six more weeks, I think to myself as I go, and I'll be cashed up and out of here.

I look up from the floor and smile briefly at the nice South African male nurse who takes the patients into surgery on the early shift. His uniform's blue and mine's an ugly mauve, clearly designating our status in the hospital pecking order, but he's still asked me to the staff Christmas party. The other cleaners, when they hear this, behave as if it's a doctor–nurse romance from Mills & Boon. They speculate on what table we'll all sit on, what they'll wear, whether there'll be door prizes this year. When I say I'm not sure if I'll go, they look at me flabbergasted.

'But it's *free*,' Dot says, 'and there's a whole three-course meal!'

'That nice young man asks you to go, I reckon you go,' says Noeleen. 'He's from overseas somewhere, isn't he? Play your cards right and you might get a trip OS!'

I'm already going overseas, I want to say to them. *I'm saving up and I might never come back.* But they're all smiling so brightly, so encouragingly, that I nod and tell them I'll be there.

And I say yes to Tony, the nurse, because of the way he holds the hands of the sore and sorry nose-job girls and tells them, 'Look at you! You're going to look gorgeous!' He turns them to blink hopefully at their woebegone, bruised reflections in their mirrors, smiling warmly over their shoulders at the transformed vision they long to see.

'Honestly,' he says, 'in a week or two you won't know yourself,' and I watch them smile back, tremulously optimistic again, under this small kindness.

Mr Moreton asks me every morning about the cigarettes.

'Please, darl,' he says. 'I'm gasping for one.'

I look at him, sitting sleeplessly in bed in his stiff new pyjamas, racked with coughing that threatens to squeeze the life out of him. He tells me the specialist has been to see him and given him the bad news, as he calls it.

'Weeks or possibly a month or two,' he says. 'You know what these fellas are like. I told him, they used to *give* us smokes in the army. They were regulation issue back then.'

I don't know what to say. 'It seems pretty ironic, doesn't it?'

'These things happen,' he says. He surveys his empty hands bleakly. 'I marched, last Anzac Day,' he adds. 'Hard to believe, isn't it?' He looks morosely out through the sealed window to the courtyard garden, where the five iceberg rosebushes struggle to survive their pruning. His fingers move restlessly against the bedsheets and each other. 'Anyhow, me daughter's coming down to see me. Bringing the grandkids.'

'Oh, that's great. When are they arriving?'

'Not sure. Tuesday, maybe. After this round of tests, anyway.'

'Mr Moreton, I'd smuggle you a cigarette — really, I would if I could. But I'm only here as a casual and they'd sack me in a minute.'

'Saving up for something, are ya?'

'To go overseas.'

'Yeah, I didn't think you were the kind of girl looking for a lifetime career cleaning tables. Not that there's anything wrong with cleaning. It's all work, isn't it?'

'Yeah, it is.'

He coughs again, and I hear the rattling undercurrent in it, like an old engine that won't turn over, a battery that's nearly flat.

'I'd kill for a smoke, though,' he says when he can speak again. 'Seriously. It's not as if they can hurt me now.'

I'm remembering my directive about fraternising, but I hate standing here beside his bed, like some official. I sit down and peel off my glove, pick up his hand. It's like a bundle of twigs. That hand, I tell myself, held a rifle, tried to stop itself trembling with terror, worked all its life.

'Are you right for everything else?' I say.

'Yep, I am. I'm right. Don't mind me.' The fingers squeeze mine.

Suddenly Marie's at the door. 'Can I see you, please?' she says, her tone like permafrost.

I stand up quickly. 'Sure,' I say breezily, smiling at Mr Moreton as I leave.

Marie's furious. The matron's seen me lingering in here and has sought her out and spoken to her.

'You clearly haven't got enough to do if you've got time to sit around annoying the patients. Here.' She thrusts a canister of cleaning powder at me, a scrubbing brush. 'You can go down and clean the old bathroom out from top to toe.'

'The what?'

'The bathroom in the Menzies wing.'

I stare at her stupidly. 'But it's about to be demolished.'

'Next week,' she snaps. She has her chin up, outraged at my inexcusable lapse, my insolence. 'Now get down there and do it and stay out of Matron's way.'

'But ...'

'She came and *found* me,' she says in an enraged whisper.

What, slacking off in the storeroom? I want to say, but instead meekly take the Ajax and brush from her and traipse down to the old bathroom. I have to step over builders' scaffolding and drop sheets to get in there, and someone's already disconnected the sinks and levered some broken tiles off the wall with a crowbar. It's ridiculous — I'm cleaning equipment that will be in the skip next week. Still, I take a deep breath and turn on the old tap to rinse out the first bath, which is so deep I have to climb into it to really scrub it clean.

I'll look back on this and laugh, I think grimly as I scour away at the rust stains. I don't owe these people anything. I can just finish in January and walk away with my three thousand dollars and my passport and get out of here.

There's a big high-pressure shower hose on the wall, and when I'm finished I swill it over the ceramic surfaces of the baths till they're gleaming, ready for the wreckers to tear out and dump. Then this wing will be rebuilt into shining private rooms, fitted out with the moulded seamless shower recesses Dot mops every day, all laminex and mirrors, all reflective surfaces everywhere. After this, I think idly, I'll go down to the function hall and polish the parquetry floor there until it's so buffed and shining that Marie will be called to account if someone takes a tumble on it at the staff Christmas party. Perhaps someone could sue her.

'I'm getting close now,' Dot tells me, waving the order form gaily at morning tea, after Noeleen's bought two bath-oil-and-moisturiser pamper packs from her catalogue.

It's a week till Christmas and I've been up a ladder, dustily hanging festive green and red bunting along the corridors and suspending plastic holly decorations in the doorways with sticky tape.

'A dab of eucalyptus oil on cotton wool,' Dot advised in passing, 'will get that off later.'

'Have you asked the scholar if she's seen anything she likes?' Noeleen says to her jokingly now, fishing in her handbag for her purse.

That's their nickname for me now, *the scholar*, ever since Dot saw me at the bus stop after work one day last week, reading a novel.

'I thought you'd finished school,' she'd said, and I'd answered, 'Yeah, I have,' and she'd stood looking at my book with a perplexed air.

'Oh,' she'd said abruptly, 'right!' almost flinching with shy goodwill.

Now I watch her carefully counting change for Noeleen out of her purse, and until this moment I've felt annoyed at this nickname and the thought of them discussing me — impatient to be in a world, instead, where reading a novel in public isn't a cause for comment.

But I suddenly change my mind. It's the purse that does it; it's so worn and well used compared to the elegant grey wallet I got for my eighteenth. That, and the care with which the two of them handle those coins.

I pull the catalogue towards me and tick boxes on the order form, adding up as I go. I reach the total which entitles Dot to the Christmas Gift Bonus. I keep ticking, until she's eligible for the coveted Gold Seller twenty-four-carat stickpin. That's two shifts' worth of salary I pull from my grey wallet, as she holds out an envelope, speechless. Ten hours of spraying and wiping, crawling on hands and knees scrubbing at rubber streaks, upending ash bins and gagging, mopping chlorine into shower recesses, mindlessly buffing laminex. That's a lot to pay for some tacky jewellery and April Violets body lotion, and we both know it as I hand over the money.

I wait around to see the look on Len's face when she tells him. His expression, I think to myself, will be worth it. Here's another mistake I make: I think Len will be chastened, satisfyingly disconcerted, forced to eat his words. When he hears, though, he is radiant with pride. As he congratulates his wife it strikes me for the first time that, with their odd shifts, this fifteen-minute tea-break is one of the few times the two of them see each other all day.

'All things going well those earrings will be here in time for you to wear them to the Christmas party,' Dot assures me.

'Terrific,' I say.

She and Len glance at each other again and grin, and I've got my money's worth, after all.

I work backwards today, from the elective-surgery ward down to the nurses' station and recreation room, because I don't want to run into the matron unless I have to.

'There you are!' says Mr Moreton when I get to his room.

'Well, at least someone's happy to see me.'

'Get a telling-off, did ya? Just for talking to an old man?'

I shrug, like it means nothing, like I'm a nonchalant girl on her way to Europe and real life.

'Don't worry about it.' I hate the way I'm keeping my voice low and furtive as I tidy up his newspaper and spray the table. 'Heard any news about your daughter coming with her kids?'

'Yeah. Tomorrow, they reckon.' He sighs, takes a quavering breath.

'What's wrong? That's good, isn't it?'

'Well,' he says, hesitating like it's my feelings that should be spared. He glances up at me, and I'm struck by the sharp blueness of his eyes. 'It is and it isn't. It'll be because they've given her the word.'

I wait, thick-headed and confused.

'She's interstate,' he says softly. 'She wouldn't come unless I was on me last legs.'

I look at him, and his bony, carved-thin shoulders rise and fall. 'I'm not complainin',' he says, his eyes on the empty garden outside. 'That's just the way it goes.'

It's easy to start work half an hour early the next day. The night staff give me tired, vague smiles as I head to the staffroom to change into my uniform, and I can just see the rim of the sun rising on the horizon like a burnished disc as I slip into Mr Moreton's room.

'What's this?' he says, blinking at his watch in the gloom when he sees me. 'It's only just gone five.'

'First cab off the rank today,' I say, and nudge the door shut with my foot. 'Man with important family visitors. Do you reckon you can get into your wheelchair?'

He looks at me. 'Of course I can.'

I feel the sinewy old muscle in his arm as he lowers himself, and the remnant strength as he leans over, hauling his breath in, to put on his own slippers. Then he sits back up, and I stow his towel and toilet bag, and we're ready.

Nobody stops us as we wheel down to the deserted Menzies wing, nobody even notices us. Mr Moreton whistles when I steer him around the scaffolding and through the door.

'Now that,' he says, 'is what I call a bath.'

I just smile as I turn on the taps and let the water thunder into the tub. Back in his room by six, I'm thinking, and no one the wiser.

'And it's so clean,' he says, shaking his head.

'I know,' I say. 'I cleaned it.'

'You little champion.'

There's an awkward silence as we both look at the steam curling off the deep, waiting water.

'I can wait outside if you'd rather, and leave you to it with the stepladder there,' I say, 'or I can give you a hand in.'

'Up to you. Don't want to embarrass you.'

'Let me give you a hand then.'

There's nothing to it in the end, just a steadying grip to help lift him up and over the rim.

In the water, he cautiously releases his hold on the sides and lets himself float outstretched, eyes closed against the rising steam. I stand there, holding his pyjamas and dressing-gown, terrified he'll have a coughing fit, or that someone will burst in.

'Do you know,' he says, 'I haven't had a bath in I don't know how long. Used to having to sit on a plastic chair in the shower. Or stand there clutching those bloody grab rails. Haven't been like this for years.'

'Like what?' I say. My heart is jumping into the back of my throat.

'Weightless,' he says finally. 'Completely weightless.'

I keep my face neutral and preoccupied as I hurry him back along the corridors to his room. He's pink-faced and loose-limbed in his fresh pyjamas and comb-ploughed damp hair.

'The doctor never puts his head in till 8 a.m. at least,' he says. 'What is it now?'

'It's 6.25,' I answer. I see a nurse passing at the end of the corridor and look down. Shouldn't have worn my mauve uniform. Should have worn my own shirt and pretended to be a relative. But nobody stops us. It's still too early.

In his room I hold the mirror while he runs his electric razor over his cheeks and chin, putting a hand to his chest to pull the slack skin on his neck taut, observing his own reflection critically as he finishes.

'You know, I never wanted to live past seventy-five,' he says, 'till the day I turned seventy-four.'

As I put away his shaver in his toilet bag I see an unopened bottle of aftershave with a sticker saying *Happy Christmas, Grandad!* still on the box. I raise my eyebrows enquiringly.

'Why not,' he says when he sees me holding it up. 'Pass it over here!'

It's the recklessness in his voice that decides me.

I help him change his pyjama top for the shirt and sweater he has hanging in his cupboard, and I hold out my hand to help him into his wheelchair again.

He looks at me shrewdly. 'Where are we going?' Looking great in his shirt and jumper, like anyone's grandfather, like someone who'll be checking out of this hospital any day now.

'AWOL,' I say. It's true too. I know as I wheel him

out the door that we're crossing the point of no return, way beyond any casual fraternising I could explain away, but nobody sees us as we pass three rooms on the way to the exit door leading to the courtyard and, anyway, I can't let him down now, not when he's shaved and changed and keeps clenching and unclenching his hands with anticipation.

It's awkward manoeuvring the two of us around to depress the lever on the door and open it, and there's a sucking sound as the airlock is broken when I lean into it. A draught of fresh air blows over us, and I worry that the cool air outside will bring on a coughing fit, but Mr Moreton takes a deep, careful breath with his face up to the weak sunlight, fumbling for the brake on the wheelchair as we reach the tanbarked square of garden, then settles his hands in his blanketed lap with a sigh.

He watches me with gleaming, expectant relish as I tap out a cigarette from the packet in my bag and pass it to him, then dig again in my bag for the lighter. When I bring its flame to the tip of the smoke in his mouth, his hand grabs mine and holds it. Then I feel the grip relax as he tilts his chin and exhales like he's been holding his breath for a long, long time. He lowers the hand with the cigarette to his knee with calm, slow relief.

'What can I say?' he whispers through a wreath of smoke. 'Your blood's worth bottling.'

I smile and check my watch, my own hands shaking. It's almost seven.

'Just don't inhale too deeply and start coughing,' I say.

'No chance of that,' he mutters, bringing the cigarette back to his lips as if he's blowing a lingering kiss. He's like a different man with a cigarette in his hand. He gazes affectionately at the rosebushes and beyond them, off to the distant hills visible between the hospital's east and south wings.

'You look very nice,' I say.

'Do I? I feel bloody great,' he says, stretching with a contented yawn, and there's a little zephyr of morning breeze that washes over us, warm and fragrant with the faint scent of blossom, and I'm about to speak again when the propped-open door slides slowly shut behind us on its hinges. There is a terrible echoing click as it closes on its own deadlock, and I recognise the sound as soon as I hear it. It is the sound of a plane door closing without me, ready to taxi down a runway and take off for London. Suddenly I very much doubt I'll be going to the staff Christmas party, either.

'Was that the door?' Mr Moreton says, his eyes fixed on the hills.

'I'm afraid so.'

'So we'll need to find another entrance?' His carefully combed, side-parted hair and the prickles of white whiskers he's missed on his face send a piercing, protective ache through me.

'Yeah. But don't worry, it'll be fine. You can take your time now.'

'Don't you worry,' he says. 'I am.'

He gives the butt one last regretful glance and throws it onto the path, where I stub it out with my toe.

'Ready when you are,' he says.

I wheel the chair to the far corner of the courtyard and down past the pathology wing, around the corner, skirting rows of garbage skips, and up the path beside accident and emergency. There's no chance of slipping through unnoticed now; the hospital's come awake and nurses and doctors are walking in briskly from the staff car park, eyeing us curiously, as I make my way past a locked door and yet another emergency exit, also locked.

'We'll have to go in via the front,' I say to Mr Moreton. 'There's no way round it.'

'Don't worry,' he says. 'I've been to the front and survived once already.' I'm laughing as he adds, 'I'm real sorry, though. You'll lose your job, won't you?'

'I couldn't care less about the job.'

'What about you going off to London and all?'

'I'll just go a bit later than I planned. It's not like it's going anywhere.'

'Sorry to make you run the gauntlet, though.'

'Nothing to apologise for,' I say.

I'm around the corner now, wheeling the chair on the long sweeping stretch of pavement leading to the black glass doors of the impressive entrance atrium. The two black ash bins stand sentinel at either side, but someone else will be hosing them out this morning.

'Here we go,' I whisper, bending to Mr Moreton's ear. The woody, clean fragrance of his Christmas aftershave makes me want to cry.

'Eyes front,' he whispers in return.

We start up the wide concourse with its landscaped box-hedge border, morning light hitting the tinted glass of the doors and heads turning to us as we approach. Mr Moreton's shoulders go back and his chin lifts and we're clipping along now, left right left, there's no way I'm going to do him the disservice of skulking in, it's up and over the top for us.

Down in the kitchen the other cleaners will be pouring their cups of tea out of the urn now, Marie remarking coolly on my absence, and Matron will be waiting for us, I am certain, at the nurses' station, in the no-man's-land of the hospital's thermostatically cool interior, its sterilised world of hard surfaces, wiped clean and blameless. Someone else's jurisdiction now.

Mr Moreton feels it, I know he does, because I hear him start humming 'It's a Long Way to Tipperary', which dissolves in a hoot of laughter then a coughing fit, and I reach down and grab his frail hand again till it's over. Then we push on, both of us smothering laughter, and this moment is the one I remember most clearly from the year I turned eighteen: the two of us content, just for this perfect moment, to believe we can go on humming, and that this path before us will stretch on forever.

Tender

Up in under her arm, that's where it aches. That's what worries her. They say the biopsy will be a minor invasive procedure, a couple of stitches at most, but she can't help thinking of that scalpel like an apple corer, going into her flesh, pushing in and twisting.

'You haven't written it on the calendar,' says Al when he comes in.

'It's at 9.15.'

'So you'll — what — get the 6.35 train?'

'Yeah, I'll drive down and leave the car at the station for you to pick up. Then back in time for after school.' She pauses, then mutters, 'Hopefully, I mean.'

'Why didn't you write it up?'

She stops grating cheese, stares at him. 'Why do you reckon?'

'Chris, the kids know. I told them last week you had to

have a test at the hospital. They're fine about it. No point making it worse for them, keeping it all secret.'

'It's not going to be worse for them. They don't even need to think about it.' She looks down at the piece of roughened cheese in her hand, turns it to a new edge.

'What do they call it again?'

'A lumpectomy.'

She hates that word. Lump. The ugliest word in the English language. *Lumpen. Lumpy*. She thinks fleetingly of the story Hannah developed an obsession for when she was three, which she'd demanded over and over, night after night. The princess with all the mattresses who still couldn't sleep because of that tiny lump disturbing her all night long; that hard, resilient pea rising cruelly and insistently through all those downy layers.

'Want a hand with something?'

'No,' she replies, taking a teatowel out of the drawer and pulling open the oven. 'I'm right.'

Hannah is off that story now. She's on to another one about a family who end up bringing two stray dogs home from the pound instead of one. Christine had fantasies when the kids were babies: of Jamie, three years older, reading to his little sister of a night in the big armchair. She'd imagined a golden halo of lamplight, polished floors, the straw-bale walls finally rendered and whitewashed, everything as clean and wholesome as a cake of handmade soap.

Instead, Jamie is forever setting up complicated wars

of small action figures that bite painfully into your bare feet when you have to get up at night, battalions of tiny medieval knights with pointy plastic armour and shields. Hannah couldn't be less interested. Christine is having a few second thoughts, now, about the old nature-versus-nurture argument. What is it with boys and fighting? One hour of sanctioned TV a night, and still Jamie sprawls on the floor relishing battle scenes, while Hannah flounces and squeals like some miniature Paris Hilton demanding to wear nail polish to kinder. Where have they absorbed all this from, this nasty flotsam leaking in like battery acid?

You couldn't have told her, seven years ago, she'd be worrying about this stuff, any more than she would have believed they'd even have a television or electric heaters.

She remembers Al and her arguing over whether to render the walls with mud and cement or just mud — statistics about toxicity, about pure environments, about every bloody thing, things that buckled in the face of practicality and time. Now the solar panels are just a booster for an electric system like everyone else's, and to Christine that seems to sum up the whole experiment: it's a bonus, a gesture, a grand theory of sustainability modified to a more prosaic reality. The trees outside, which she'd imagined sprouting into a shady arbour, are taller and stalkier now but still unmistakably seedlings, painstakingly hand-watered from the dam and the bath. The piles of clay turned over by digging the house site still glint exposed through the thin groundcovers, and Jamie's BMX track has worn a looping circuit through the landscaping, turning her plans for terracing into an assortment of jumps and scrambles. Christine puts more wood in the firebox and, with a familiar mix of guilt and resentment, dreams her nightly dream of an electric oven.

It's not that she doesn't love the house. She does — it's just still so makeshift and unfinished. The spare windows are still stacked under a tarp in the shed, and they've spread rugs over the spots where the floor dips and cracks. You can't have a bath without bucketing out the water saved from the last one onto some dry patch of ground.

She can hear Al giving the kids a bath now. That's Al's version of a fun activity with kids — stick them in the bath and try to foam up some bubbles with the biodegradable shampoo.

'Mum!' she hears Hannah bawling from the tub.

'What?'

'I need my SHOWER CAP!'

'Get Dad to find it.'

Now Al's voice, muffled and distracted. 'It's not in here.'

'Have you looked in the shower?'

She hears the shower screen door open, then silence, a belated muttered thanks. Too late though.

'My hair's ALL WET ALREADY!' comes Hannah's wail, followed by that whiny crying that always sets

Christine's teeth on edge. Does Hannah do it at kinder? Do the workers there tut and roll their eyes about lack of discipline at home?

'Shut UP!' comes Jamie's voice.

Violent splashing, then another high-pitched scream.

Why doesn't Al do something to intervene? She pulls open the big drawer with an irritated tug and gets out knives and forks.

Al had been the first one she'd told, of course, after she'd found it, late one night in the shower. She recalls his face as he raised himself on one elbow in bed, reaching for his bedside lamp, how he'd rubbed a hand over his eyes, pinching the bridge of his nose between thumb and forefinger. Then the radiographer: how quiet she'd got, after the initial small talk. Christine remembers the sharply intent way she'd leaned her head closer to the image on the screen, her hand clicking, moving the mouse, clicking again, the light-hearted talk over.

Then the doctor, finally, looking through the ultrasound films as he made a point of giving her the reassuring statistics of how many lumps turn out to be benign. She'd hated the way he'd stared off over her head as his fingers had coolly explored the lump, gazing into the distance like someone solving a mental equation.

'How does that feel?' he'd said.

'Pretty tender, actually.' Trying to breathe normally.

Him writing something on her card, like his final

answer in a quiz, before meeting her eyes again. Briskness and neutrality finetuned, as he said, 'Best to take that out and have a good look at it, I think.'

Christine sits at the kitchen table now and listens to the wrangling in the bathroom, her husband's ineffectual protestations as the children fight over a certain squeaky bath toy they both lay claim to. From out of the corner of her eye, she sees the familiar tiny dark shape of a mouse run the length of the skirting. If she puts another trap out, she'll have to remember to tell Al to check them before the kids get up tomorrow. Finding a dead mouse is likely to set them both off, demanding a funeral and burial, which would make them late for school.

She gets up and finds two traps in the pantry, in behind the jars and plastic containers and the box full of herbal cough and cold remedies, valerian tea and rescue remedy. Back when the kids were born, she and Al would never have dreamed of treating them with any commercial preparations from the chemist. And they'd been lucky: the kids never got sick; she hadn't been in a hospital since Hannah was born.

Rescue remedy, she thinks as she replaces the little bottle on the shelf. And can't stop her mouth twisting into a humourless, cynical curl as she dabs some peanut butter onto the mousetraps and sets them, pushing them cautiously back into shadowy corners with the tip of her finger.

'Al!' she calls at last. 'Will you get the kids out of the bath, for God's sake? Dinner's been ready for half an hour!'

She finds herself watching him, sometimes, still a little incredulous at the dreamy way he handles life, how everything seems to flow around him. Once at a barbeque held at the community centre where he works, she'd impulsively asked a colleague how he managed everything there at the office.

'Oh, fine,' the woman had said, surprised. 'Al just does his own thing, you know? It all comes together in the end.'

Here at home, she never sees it coming together. Everything, on the contrary, seems to be teetering on the verge of coming apart. That, or just sinking into neglect, like the wheelbarrow half-full of compost and the shovel which has been buried in weeds for over a fortnight, outside the kitchen window.

He never rises to the bait, either. Once, when he'd wandered in from the study and said, 'What have you got planned for dinner?' she'd snapped, 'What have *you* got planned?' but he'd only looked surprised and answered mildly, 'Nothing. Is it my turn?'

He only makes one dinner, though: tuna and pasta casserole. Christine supposes she should be grateful he's so laid-back — relaxed with the kids, always in the same amiable mood. But he's so vague, that's the trouble, so blind to how much *organising* she has to do around him to keep it all running. It's like she has three kids, not two.

Now she watches him dump clean folded clothes out of the washing basket onto the rug, slowly picking through the pile looking for fresh pyjamas for the kids.

'Hurry, Dad! Hurry!' whines Hannah, jiggling naked and impatient on the spot.

Christine drinks in the sight of her strong little back, the sturdy muscles in her legs as she jumps from one foot to the other.

Al looks up at Hannah and raises his eyebrows, tickles her with one teasing forefinger. 'Don't get your knickers in a twist,' he says, and Jamie guffaws with laughter at his sister, who complains even louder and kicks out at him. He aims his Jedi fighter plane warningly at her. Al doesn't even notice. He glances down at the pyjama top he's holding and with one distracted but surprisingly adept movement reaches his hand inside to the label and shakes it right-way-out.

If they do the tests in the afternoon, Christine wonders, will they keep her down there tomorrow night if the results are bad? She tries the word in her head, exploratively, trying to take the terrifying sting out of it. *Malignant. Malignant.* Would they be so prompt, or would some other specialist have to make the decision? Does she have tuna and pasta in the pantry, just in case?

'I need a cardboard box,' Jamie announces after dinner, 'for my school project.'

Christine finds him an old four-litre wine cask.

'What's this for?' she asks as he cuts a hole in one end.

'We're making models. It's going to be a little world, kind of. Like, I'm going to put blue paper in here, for sky? And some little sticks like trees. And when people look through the hole it's going to look like a real place.'

'Wow, that sounds good. When does it have to be ready?'

'Tomorrow,' he replies calmly.

God, sometimes he's so like Al it scares her.

'Shall we go and cut some sticks and twigs, then?' she suggests.

He glances out at the twilight and shrugs. 'OK.'

'What are you going to stick them in, to make them stand up?'

She watches his serious seven-year-old face consider this, and wants to take his arm and plant a kiss on the faded temporary tattoo of Buzz Lightyear there on his skinny bicep.

'Playdough,' he says at last.

'Right.'

'Covered in grass so you can't see it.'

She feels the ardent rush of helpless, terrible love. 'Let's do it.'

She feels it catch, like a little stabbing stitch, when she reaches up to snip off some wattle sprigs. In the armpit again, like it's buried in her lymph nodes instead of the pale, pliant skin at the side of her breast. She'd been showering when she first felt it six weeks ago, soaping herself after a dusty day collecting bricks for paving. Her fingers had brushed over it, and she'd felt her pulse leap and thud, racketing to the roof of her mouth, and traced her fingers back to the tender place, tasting sudden adrenaline like solder. Yes, like a pea, buried but resilient, a small sly sphere nesting disguised between layers of flesh and tissue. Keeping you awake all night. Wondering how long it'd been there unnoticed, and what it might be collecting darkly into itself, like a little Death Star.

'What colour playdough?' she asks now, squeezing her arm next to her side, breathing deeply. 'Are you going to do stars or clouds?'

As she makes tomorrow's lunches she watches Jamie at the kitchen table, assembling what he needs, pasting a pale sky inside the box with a gluestick as his tongue jerks across his bottom lip in concentration.

'How long have you had this project?' grumbles Al when Jamie is nowhere near finished at bedtime. 'You should have started it earlier.'

Al, whose half-finished bookshelves they all step over on the way to the carport, who leaves the wet washing in the basket at the line while he drives into town for more pegs, who can't seem to shut a drawer once he's opened it.

'You really do have to get to bed soon,' Christine says to Jamie.

His face goes mutinous. 'There's these other kids,' he says as he pats chopped grass clippings down, 'who always have their things ready on time? Always on the first day? Tomorrow they'll have theirs finished.'

He stares down disconsolately at the box and reaches in suddenly for the little plastic soldiers he's arranged in combat inside. 'Got to take these out,' he mutters. 'These aren't right.'

Warmth blooms briefly in her chest, tight and aching like tears.

'Ten more minutes,' orders Al, who wants the kids in bed so he can surf the net on the computer he'd once sworn he'd never own.

Everything's quiet by the time Christine finds a packet of icy-pole sticks in the kitchen drawer. Jamie has gone to bed resignedly, and Al is in some chatroom, off in his study. On the table lies the box, some cotton-wool balls for clouds waiting till morning. She can imagine Jamie gluing them on as he shovels cereal into his mouth, how studious and intent his face will be. She'll be on the train by then, the city a polluted Gotham on the distant horizon.

Well, maybe she can surprise him. She reaches inside the packet and breaks three icy-pole sticks in half and digs the pieces into the playdough to make a perfect little fence in the box. When you look through the eyehole it's like a diorama, one of those stagy, rustic sets from *The Wizard of Oz*. She arranges some grass around the bases, then glues some of the sticks together and sets them on an angle like a part-opened gate.

Look at me, she grins to herself, shaking her head. *I'm turning into one of those parents who take over their kids' school projects.*

In the back of the wardrobe she finds an old handbag and removes a small mirror, which she arranges semi-buried in the grass, like a little reflective pond. Pokes the wattle sprigs around it, bending like she-oaks by the water.

It's 10.30 now. She catches another little galloping mouse-shadow in her peripheral vision, running across the kitchen floor into the pantry to disappear in behind the recycled paper and compost bucket, and she moves to set yet another mousetrap inside a cupboard. No wonder they sell the things in packs of six. She's back sitting at the kitchen table before she even realises, ducking her head to squint through the hole in the box. The trick is going to be letting enough light in the roof to simulate real sunshine. She hunts in a bag of Christmas wrapping in the hall cupboard and finds a square of yellow cellophane, cuts it to size and fits it between the layers of cardboard like a skylight. With the desk lamp she checks how the light will look. Golden afternoon sun pouring over an

Enid Blyton countryside. Magic hour.

Al comes in yawning, sees her and chortles.

'Don't even start,' she says. 'I can't help myself.'

He puts the kettle on. 'Hey, remember that papier-mâché volcano on display at parent–teacher night, that we were all meant to believe had been made by a kid in Grade 2?' He laughs again at the memory, scratching his head as he gets two cups out and starts stacking the plates to wash up.

'I'm imagining the surprise when he comes down tomorrow,' she says. 'But if I ever go any further than this, tell me.'

Al dunks a glass in the sink. 'Don't worry about tomorrow, OK?' he says, after a while. 'I'm sure everything will work out fine.'

She doesn't look up, but she senses him standing there with his back to her, washing the glass until it's way beyond clean.

Getting on for midnight. She sits back and stretches. Sand, that's what she needs. To glue round the edges of the mirror, to simulate a shore. She steps outside and takes a few pinches from the dark pile next to the paving bricks. One thing about living in a house like this: raw materials are never far away. She glues a wavy, natural line around the mirror, and sticks on some dry stalks like reeds, holding them in place with tweezers as they dry.

She knows Hannah's got some black plasticine somewhere, for some swans. Maybe in her toy box, or in her little desk? She creeps into her daughter's room, and stands listening to the rhythmic steadiness of Hannah's breathing, gazes at her sprawled sideways on the bed as if she's just landed from a great height. Hannah: healthy, respiring, her cells a blur of miraculously multiplying and flowering growth, life coursing through her, flawless, down to the last crescent-moon fingernail.

Christine, who once slept with a hand cupped around that tiny kicking foot, praying for a safe delivery, now stands holding scissors and a page of silver stars, making impossible bargains at the speed of light. Her own heart knocking in her chest and something else, something dark and airless, trickling through her bloodstream, that black, dense shadow on the ultrasound searching for somewhere to colonise. Her feet take her into Jamie's room and she stands gazing at him too. Her children, perfect, made with her own once-trustworthy body.

She gets up, silently, at five, nagged by an unfinished vision and the sensation of the night draining away. Out in the garden she's calm again, feeling the dew drench her ankles and the bottom of her white cotton nightdress. She can sleep on the train, anyway. She walks slowly through the hillocks and raised beds, seeing her nightdress billow like a faintly luminous ghost, pausing to inhale the deep spicy smell of the lemon-scented gum. She sees Jamie in the morning, milky-breathed and drowsy, finding the box, looking through the eyehole with a shock of pleasure, being finished early for once in his life.

She glances up at the house. Yellow light in the square window, her family sleeping warm and secure. She clutches the sprig of Chinese elm she's found, which will look just like an apple tree, and crouches by the pile of paving stones. Her fingers search blindly into the damp crevices of the stack. Somewhere in here, she knows, is some moss; cool and velvety, perfect for the distant green hills behind the open gate in that little microcosmic landscape.

She'll leave it at his place at the table, ready. And their lunchboxes packed at the front of the fridge, where Al won't miss them. For some reason, she keeps recalling Al, suddenly surprising her by shaking those pyjamas right-way-out with that one deft easy motion. She can't think why, but the image comforts her.

Back inside, the dawn light reaching the kitchen, she checks the time again: thirty minutes till the train, just over three hours till she's in that doctor's room again. She looks out the unpainted window at their little patch of bush, and at what's becoming visible out there — the ridges of hard clay subsoil showing palely defiant through the grass, like a healing scar.

Then, cold but wide awake and ready, she locates each of the five mousetraps she's set and kneels down in front of each of them in turn. Carefully, with the flat of her hand, she releases the springs so that the small metal trays of bait slip from the jagged hook holding them in place. She's humming to herself as she grasps each straining metal bar and guides it back to let it settle, with a benign and harmless snap, against the small rectangle of wood.

Like a House on Fire

First, the humiliation of purchase, in which I am forced to watch my wife and eldest son, aged eight, lugging the Christmas tree we've just bought to our car. The Rotary guy, who's sold it to me off the back of his truck in the supermarket car park, gives me a look he reserves for shirkers, layabouts, vandals and those destroying the social fabric by refusing to pull their weight.

'Back injury,' I say to him, and he watches the two of them hefting it onto the roof of the station wagon, and just says, 'Right.' Behind him, the graffiti outside Subway reads, *Only eight shoplifting days till Christmas*, which under normal circumstances I would photograph or at least point out to Claire, except she's busy passing rope through the open windows of the car, exaggeratedly checking her watch because she starts a shift in half an hour.

When we get home she lugs the tree into the lounge room and mutters, 'I have to go.'

Very little eye contact these days, my wife. This is my fourth month off work with what my first doctor diagnosed as a compressed disc, a condition I have since heard described as a herniated disc, a ruptured disc, a bulging disc and, naturally, the good old slipped disc. Only two things to do if you don't want surgery, and that's rest and take fistfuls of anti-inflammatories and, of course, fail each week to bring home any sort of pay cheque. Claire clocks off from her hospital job, caring for helpless people who also lie down a lot, and comes straight back home to me.

That Saturday afternoon I do the very thing I'd promised my physio fifteen weeks ago I wouldn't do: namely, pull down the attic ladder after Claire's left and try dragging the boxes and bundles of Christmas tree ornaments out of storage. I reach for the two boxes and grasp them in my arms, then when I put my foot down to descend I feel nothing but empty air beneath me where there should be a rung, making me instantly panic and let go of the boxes, both hands reflexively grabbing at the ladder. Even the jarring as my foot bangs safely down on the rung below sends a jolt up through me, a warning jolt. A 1.8 tremor on the Richter scale.

The two boxes drop like stones and I can hear the assortment of ornaments inside crunch as they hit the floor. I stand still, letting a further loose tangle of lights and tinsel rain down from the attic and upon my head, and when everything that can possibly fall has finished falling, I step gingerly off the ladder and sneak a forensic glance into the smaller box to see that the whole ceramic nativity scene is shattered. The three wise men, who'd been fitted with unnerving false eyelashes so they look like they're sashaying off to Mardi Gras rather than Bethlehem, are smashed to shards. Every sheep and cow, every adoring shepherd, broken. Only the baby Jesus in his crib, one leg raised in that classic nappy-changing pose, remains miraculously unscathed.

'Don't look,' I say to the kids as I carry the box into the living room like it's a cardboard coffin. 'I've broken everything except the baby.'

Now for the humiliation of decorating, a pretence of decorating. The Christmas tree is where they've left it — lying on the floor next to the bucket of sand — and the three kids are all glued to the TV, something that's been happening a lot since I've been the chief childcare provider, although I don't know what Claire expects me to do when I have to spend hours at a time horizontal, staring up at the ceiling. The two boys look briefly at me then back to the screen, shrugging.

'Turn that off,' I say. 'We're meant to be decorating the Christmas tree.'

My eldest, Ben, swallows a mouthful of sandwich and mutters, still gazing at the TV, 'It's only Evie that wants to.'

'Is that right? What about you, Sam? Don't you want to do it?'

'Nup.' A quick glance at his older brother for confirmation. Sam, who last year was worried about wetting the bed on Christmas Eve in case Santa saw it. Evie looks up at me with an anxious four-year-old's eyes, sitting on the couch already holding the tree fairy in her lap. They are eyes, it strikes me, that are all too familiar with endlessly compromised plans, as if life is already revealing itself to her as a long trail of small disappointments and changeable older brothers.

'Come on, turn that off and let's do it,' I say.

Ben slides me a flat glance. 'You do it,' he says. Eight years old and a voice perfected into grating delinquent surliness.

The thing is I can't, and he knows it. I can't even pick the tree up by myself.

'Get up, both of you,' I bark, 'and stand that bloody Christmas tree in the bucket! And the TV's not going back on till every last piece of tinsel is in place, do you understand me?'

I grab the remote to switch the screen off, then put it on the top of the bookshelf out of reach. That motion, swinging and lifting my arm to full stretch, feels like someone has taken a big ceramic shard out of the box — a remnant bit of shepherd, maybe, or a shattered piece of camel — and is stabbing it into the base of my spine.

'Don't worry, Evie,' I say after a few moments. I need

one ally, at least. 'They'll do it.'

And I grit my teeth and help twist the tree down into the sand after the boys have sullenly dumped it into the bucket and found bricks to anchor it. Then I watch as they put up the decorations, shifting my weight from foot to foot, sweating with the pain, just to make sure I well and truly kill the occasion now that I've poisoned it. If Claire was here, she could be the one to lift Evie up to put the fairy in place, but Claire is shovelling mashed potato into the mouths of bedridden old people for $12.50 an hour, and I can feel my daughter hovering behind me, all fourteen impossible kilos of her, and I mentally run through whether I can brace myself enough to lift her up to head height to do it, whether I still have the upper body strength. When I finally psych myself up to do it, though, I turn to see she's not holding the fairy, she's holding a cushion.

'Here, Dad,' she says. 'Lie down on the floor.'

I go to the spot I always do, like a beaten dog. Next to the couch, where I can lower or raise myself gradually by levering myself onto it, where I lie each day and dread a phone call or a sneeze.

I have sunk to my knees, nearly there in that blessed prone position when Sam blurts, 'Dad! Wait! What about the remote?'

I continue my slow swan dive towards the floor. 'Ben, climb up the bookcase shelves and get it,' I grunt, my voice preoccupied with enduring the next ten seconds. 'Don't pretend you don't know how.'

Oh, Merry Christmas, father of the year.

'Immobilisation,' the physio had said all those weeks ago, writing a list in point form down on a pad. 'Gentle stretching to help relieve pressure on the nerve root. Ice and heat packs if they help. Non-steroidal anti-inflammatories. Possibly chiropractic manipulation.'

He'd clicked his plastic model spine back and forth in his hands. 'L3, that's you there,' he said, pointing to the disc in question.

Yep, that's me there. Some days it feels like that's my entire identity focused there in one single space between two injured segments of a bone puzzle, shrunk down to one locus of existence, and seized there.

'Dad broke the nativity scene,' says Ben as soon as Claire gets home. I hear her close the front door then come down the hall, glancing in to see me in my accustomed place on the floor.

'What? How did he do that?'

'He dropped it.'

'Bloody hell. Give me a look.'

Footsteps, muttering, the sound of fingers stirring through ceramic debris. A tightly constrained hiss of frustration and fury. You get good at listening to sounds in a household when you're prone; it gets so you can almost hear a head shaking in pained disbelief, or distant teeth grinding in the silence following the lifting of the washing-machine lid and finding the clothes set on 'wash' this morning still there, strangled and spun around the agitator, and a husband who can't pull things out and can't hang things up.

Claire comes in and stands in the doorway, eyeing me.

'Can I get you anything?'

'Two ibuprofen, if you wouldn't mind.'

She trudges away — the accusation you can hear in a trudge, you wouldn't credit it — and brings me back the painkillers and a glass of water.

'How was your shift?'

'How do you think? Same as always.'

A big pause.

'It's triple pay if I work overnight on Christmas Eve.'

We let that one hang. There's just no entry point to that excruciating discussion.

'I'm getting Evie to bed then,' she says, and I hear her knees crack as she gets up.

'I've been listening to the boys playing that computer game upstairs for at least an hour, so don't believe them if they say otherwise,' I add as she heads out the door, and that's the extent of how we communicate these days, in the tiny squeezed and inflamed gap somewhere between slippage and rupture.

She's a nurse, so obviously she was lavish in her care those first few weeks. Unstinting.

'Six weeks,' she'd said encouragingly, slinging a heat pack into the microwave. 'I've been talking with the doctor at the hospital and he says there's no reason why you shouldn't recuperate fully and be up and about in six weeks. Just rest and take it easy. And,' she added, tucking the heat pack under my back, straightening up the blanket, 'yours was only mild, wasn't it? Only a mildly herniated disc?'

'Well ... yeah.' How to explain the pain, the fear of the pain, the grabbing freeze at any sudden movement? Then the weeks of me lying on the blue yoga mat, Claire on her laptop trawling the internet for information, calling, 'Any tingling and numbness in the buttocks?'

'If there's numbness, how would I know if there's also tingling?'

A long while has passed since we'd made jokes about buttocks. I can't remember the last time my wife touched me with hands that were anything except neutral and businesslike; hands turning me carefully over, carefully but somehow not gently, hands which so clearly conveyed that they wished themselves gone.

It was a side to her I was seeing for the first time, this professional, acquired distance. At our house, in our script, Claire was the slapdash one, laughing at me when I patiently restacked the dishwasher more neatly or tucked the sheets in properly. She was as messy as the kids, and that's saying something. 'They're kids,' she'd say. 'Don't inflict your perfectionism on them, for God's sake.

Leave it for your job.'

Which was how I'd always been, managing a team of workers who did tree-felling and hedge-clipping, at a point in my career where I never did any of this myself, just organised crews and timetables and equipment hire and safety requirements, so I can't even blame good honest labour for injuring my back. I'd just finished supervising a job of clipping around tennis courts in a huge formal garden up in the hills, and the owner was about to stroll out and check our handiwork, and I saw — you can see where this is going, can't you — an errant bit of cypress bough just at head height, offending my perfectionist streak. And it only takes thirty seconds to wreck a perfect safety record, and I used mine walking to the van as I cursed the new guy, picking up the heavy-duty hedge-clippers that were nearest. I jerked the start cord angrily and swung them up over my head to cut that one pointless, unobtrusive bit of stray greenery. Picking up, and lifting; you wouldn't think that would do anything like the damage of, say, falling. But I was stiff and pissed off, with something to prove, my arms going up in an arc and then instantly down again as I staggered and the blades of the hedge-cutter stuttered themselves into the dirt, something hotly molten cracking open in my back and eating its way up my spine into the pain centre at the base of my head, turning everything white.

So it's been me, using up my own scrupulous work cover as sick leave, insurance that's already expired and the half-pay remainder that's running out very, very soon in the new year, when my doctor will look at my MRI again and say — and this is my worst, darkest fantasy — 'Sixteen *weeks*? Frankly, I can't quite see why this hasn't resolved itself by now.'

There is plenty of time to relive those thirty seconds, here on the floor surrounded by toys and mess I can't pick up and driven mad by forgotten plates of toast crusts left on the coffee table. The immobilising pain of moving holds me completely still, and the scalding moments leading up to slipping the disc are on continuous repeat play, as I explore the million alternate universes that allow me to find the secateurs instead, or reach up and snap the twig off, or tuck it into the hedge and make a joke with the new guy, or just leave the bloody thing alone. Allow me, in a nutshell, to let it go. I am well aware of what's keeping me pinioned here, the compressed, pinched thing that commands all my attention now. I stare at the cornices, the tumbleweeds of fluff accumulating under the table, the faint cobweb hanging from the ceiling in a floating, dust-collecting drift. Soon we will have mice, I think. Soon rodents will invade the house and step over me, sneering, on their way to that discarded toast.

'I hate to say it,' I say to Claire when she comes in to collapse into an armchair, 'but there's a cobweb hanging from the ceiling that's really bothering me.'

'Is there?' she says brusquely, opening the TV guide. 'Good.'

They keep you awake, the anti-inflammatories. You could lie there for hours, thinking about what that sort of comment is all about.

'Christmas presents,' I say instead. 'I'm worried ...'

'It's all done,' she answers. 'I got everything yesterday in my lunch hour.'

'What? All of it?'

'Yep. I'm going to leave the wrapping up to you, though. You can sit and wrap big light boxes filled with plastic junk, can't you? Hospital corners, and all?'

'Yes, sure. Sure. It's actually feeling pretty good now.'

'Good,' she says automatically, in a tone that says *so it bloody should*, unless that's the medication making me paranoid as well as sleepless.

'Sorry about the nativity scene,' I say. 'It's Claire's, that set. Something she's had ever since she was a child.

'That's OK. It was made in the Philippines. Funny how everything except the Jesus broke.' She laughs. 'Anyway, Evie's improvising. Check out the dining-room table.'

I hoist myself up slowly and hobble over to see the crib surrounded by toys; Christmas designed by Disney and Mattel. Barbie is the Virgin Mary, Postman Pat has joined Ernie and Bert as stand-ins for the Three Wise Men. I count four shepherds, only one of which is a panda, and take in the plastic farm collection and a squadron of My Little Ponies, a giantess Dora the Explorer who must be the angel — everything replaced except, in the middle of it all, the baby with the Napoleon kiss-curl, arms spread to receive the gifts, or else to declare: *Come and adore me!*

'Don't do the Christmas Eve shift,' I say.

'There's no way round it. I have to.'

I stand there thinking of last Christmas, when we were finishing a big commercial contract and I had a pile of overtime on my pay cheque, and Claire and I, reckless and laughing at the mall, spending it like water, bought them all bikes and a trampoline and then had that week at the beach. I get down on my hands and knees in dogged slow motion, like an old-age pensioner who's dropped something.

'What are you doing?'

'One of Sam's tennis shoes is under the couch and I've been forced to look at it all afternoon and I'm going to finally pull the damn thing out.'

'Look,' she says, 'either tell Sam to get it out, or forget about it. Just give the martyrdom and control freakery a rest.'

I'm genuinely shocked. 'Control freakery, is it?'

'When it's coming from someone lying flat on their back in the middle of a busy family room, it morphs pretty quickly into orders. I mean, why *there*? Just where you can keep your eye on everything, like Central Control?'

I dangle myself over the arm of the lounge chair, stretching my spine, face in a cushion.

'I'm sorry,' I say, my voice muffled. 'I just can't stand all this … chaos I can't do anything about.'

'Well, get out and go for a walk. The doctor said gentle exercise is good. Anyway …' She hesitates. I breathe in the cottony cushion smell. 'It should be better now. It really should. There's no explanation for why it's gone on like this.'

'No. Well, Claire, I have no explanation either. I'm not faking it, if that's what you're getting at.'

'I'm not saying you're faking it, for crying out loud. Why would you put us all through this?'

I take a breath to start in on how what they're going through is nothing compared to what going through it with a herniated disc at L3 is like, having your kids step over you obliviously on the way to the TV, not knowing what's going on at work, shifting your previously reliable body around like an unexploded bomb. I imagine saying all this muffled into a cushion like someone in a '70s therapy group, then … let it go.

Instead, I put my hand down behind the cushion and feel around for the small, pointy plastic thing that's been digging into my face. 'Look, one of Evie's Polly Pocket dolls.'

Claire holds out her hand. 'I bet she's been looking for that. That's probably another shepherd.'

After she's in bed, I go to her laptop to check whether gentle exercise is a good thing. I type in *back pain* and it lists all her previous searches containing those words. The latest one is *back pain psychosomatic*. Hey, thanks, Claire.

Two more painkillers, and I get each of those crappy presents wrapped so neat and perfect and pintucked, it's like I have a degree in it. It's like I've been in the army for years, drilling myself on just this thing, in preparation for a surprise attack.

Now the humiliation of helplessness, the hands-down winner of all humiliations, after all, as on Christmas Eve I watch Claire scrape her hair back into a ponytail and put on those squeaky white shoes, ready to go to work until 5 a.m.

'I should have a to-do list,' I say, 'and I'm really, really sorry I haven't got one. It would involve taking the kids to carols by candlelight and stuffing a turkey and making you breakfast in bed tomorrow morning.'

Claire stares at herself in the mirror and grimaces, then grabs a lipstick and slicks some on. 'Well, it can't be helped,' she says, and there it is, the sound of everything she's really talking about, echoing in the big, hollow silence under her words.

Listening to the two of us, you'd never believe that we used to get on like a house on fire, that even after we had the kids, occasionally we'd stay up late, just talking. But now that I think of it, a house on fire is a perfect description for what seems to be happening now: these flickering small resentments licking their way up into the wall cavities; this faint, acrid smell of smoke. And suddenly, before you know it, everything threatening to go roaring out of control. Here's my wife with the hose, running to douse burning embers falling from a sky raining more and more embers on her, battling to save what she's got. And what am I? The guy who can't get the firetruck started? The one turning and turning the creaking tap, knowing the tank is draining empty, the one with the taste of ash in his mouth and all this black and brittle aftermath?

Once she leaves, I shuffle around the kitchen making dinner.

'Remember last year, Dad,' says Sam, 'you made those pancakes?'

'I do. But we're not having pancakes, we're having delicious pasta.'

It wouldn't kill me to make pancakes. Except that I've succumbed to this reduced, curtailed movement, all this pinched, seized stiffness where everything is such an effort.

'How do reindeers fly?' says Evie, out of nowhere.

I study the noodles in the saucepan, the grated cheese melting on them.

'Yeah, Dad,' says Ben, grinning that smart-arse eight-year-old grin. 'I've got a few questions about those flying reindeer myself.'

'Oh, I'm sure you have, Ben.'

I think, with a sudden aching spasm, of the year before, when Claire and I had read his note to Santa. *How are you*, the note said, *and how is Mrs Claus?*

'And how does Santa get into houses where there's no chimney? And how did he carry our trampoline in his sack?'

'Ben, I'd appreciate it if you thought for a second before you continued with this.'

The other two are staring at him with wide hungry eyes. He falters. I see it.

'They must be special reindeer,' he says finally. 'He breeds them.'

'An excellent answer,' I say.

'After dinner, can we cook marshmallows over a candle?' says Evie.

'I don't see why not.'

Definition of psychosomatic: something originating in the mind or the emotions rather than through a physical cause. On the website I clicked on, there was a whole theory about how low oxygen content in the nerve and muscle cells is the true cause of most chronic pain syndromes. They hasten to point out that this doesn't make the pain imaginary, just redirected via some different circuit, I guess. So I eat charred marshmallows tasting of scented Santa candles and say, 'Mmm, these are terrific,' and when I get the camera to take a photo of Evie's nativity scene, I see it now includes Transformer robots standing around the crib like bodyguards, and I say, 'They look *great*, Sam. This is about the best nativity scene I've ever seen.'

Then Ben reaches over and puts Darth Vader in the

place of Joseph, and wheezes asthmatically, 'Jesus, I am your *father*,' and laughing feels like panting for breath, remembering what it's like to be fit.

At 1 a.m. I tackle the stairs up to their bedrooms, pausing halfway to allow plenty of oxygen into my nerve and muscle cells, timing my dose of anti-inflammatories but feeling hot pain building anyway, unstoppable. I grope my way in the darkness towards their beds and the sacks hanging off them with the armful of small, perfectly wrapped stocking-stuffers my wife has bought on her credit card.

'Hi, Santa.' Ben's not asleep. He shifts in the bunk bed to squint at me in the dim moony glow of the night-light.

'Good evening,' I say. My voice comes out more resonant than I would have expected, considering I'm holding on to the doorjamb in a grabbing spasm, sweat trickling down my neck.

There's a short pause in which he could choose to wake his brother.

'You're looking fitter than I would have thought,' is what he says.

'Well, I keep in shape. Lots of stairs in this line of work.'

'Reindeers OK?'

I have to bite the inside of my cheek. 'Excellent, thanks.'

'And Mrs Claus?'

Pain originating in the mind or the emotions — I'm clear on that now. It still locks like brakes, forcing you to skid to a stop. I gesture with the DVD I'm about to put into his Santa sack. 'Doesn't like me working nights. Lucky it's just the one night, I guess.'

He laughs softly, so he doesn't wake Sam. 'Will Mum be here in the morning?'

'Yep.'

'Goodnight, then.'

'See you, Benny boy.'

You'll think I'm insane when I tell you I make it back downstairs again just to turn around and work my teeth-gritted way back up again. My physio would roll his eyes and shake his head if I confessed. Especially if I said I climbed back up those stairs for no good reason, other than to get another look at each of them asleep, sprawled in their beds without a worry in the world. He's twenty-six, my physio, and not a father, so it's understandable, I guess.

This whole mind/body somatic thing has got me spooked, so don't think the irony hasn't occurred to me that I can only get comfortable if I lie flat on my back, like the infant Saviour, with one leg raised. I wake up at 5.30 when Claire comes in quietly, and through the doorway, I watch her unloading stuff from the all-night supermarket in the kitchen: two barbeque chickens, a bag of potato gems, one of those seven-dollar ice-cream desserts with the crackly chocolate inside the kids love. She's right, I can see everything from here: the dining-room table arranged with its galaxy of plastic and soft-toy worshippers, swirling around the unbroken Jesus like a constellation. The white cloth we only use at Christmas, with the centrepiece of something glued with curly pasta and spray-painted gold that Evie made at kindergarten. Over there, the stairs they will come down in a couple of hours, to step over me on their way to the tree.

'Will you do me a favour?' I call to Claire, and she comes over, picking up one of Santa's shortbreads on the way and cramming it sideways into her mouth. 'You remember that time I got a stiff neck on holidays, when you showed me that back-cracking trick?'

'Um, yeah. But I'm not sure your physio would recommend it in your current state, would he?'

'He mentioned gentle pressure. And that's kind of what a chiropractor does, isn't it?'

'I'm not a chiropractor, though.' She swallows the biscuit. 'You were on holidays with a cricked neck, not recovering from a slipped disc.'

'Go on. Don't tell me you wouldn't love to walk all over me.'

She gives a brief, weary grin. 'Oh, no, that part would be my pleasure.' She gets two chairs and lines them up either side of me and kicks off her shoes as I roll myself onto my front.

'Forehead and shoulders on the floor,' she says. She grips the backs of the chairs and braces herself against them, and I feel her sure foot, bare and warm, align itself squarely between my shoulder blades.

'Breathe in and out,' she says, and then begins to press with slow careful weight, down onto my back. I feel her hesitate, like someone testing ice before stepping out onto it, and I hear her say, 'Well, maybe this isn't doing you much good, but it's working for me,' and I smile into the floor, in spite of myself, feeling my sternum take the pressure. I exhale another cautious breath as her heel pushes a fraction harder and finds the spot and something cracks — we both hear it — like a flexed knuckle. A candle-flare passes up my back, flickering, moth-like.

'There it goes,' she says, lifting her weight gently off me.

'Thank you,' I say, and she crouches beside me and brings her face down next to mine.

'Temporary respite,' she says. 'Happy Christmas.'

I look at her, feeling that small heat build between us. Our breaths fuelling it, close to the ground. This is how you do it, I think, stick by careful stick over the ashes, oxygen and fuel, a controlled burn. I open my mouth to tell her sorry.

Then I blink and refocus, distracted, and see, behind her in the greyish dawn, a line of ground-in glitter and stars stuck in the carpet. Probably with glue.

'Look at that,' I say, and she turns her head from floor height to see what I'm talking about.

'What?' she says, mystified.

'Those stars. There.'

'Oh … yes! Don't they look great, in this light,' she says, and I reach up to pull the elastic band and grips out of her hair.

Five-Dollar Family

'This is the most important meal of your baby's life.'

Michelle had opened her eyes, groggy and aching after the birth, and seen the midwife's stern face loom into view over her. 'What?'

'You've got to wake him up every three hours, remember? You've got a sleepy baby, and you've got to make him interested in feeding so that he gets all the antibodies he needs from you. And also to make your milk come in.'

She's the bossy one. The other one is nicer, the one who was on duty the morning after and asked Michelle how she was going. That was all — no looking at her stitches, no lectures, just how she was. Then she'd picked Jason up, unwrapped him, and passed him gently to Michelle.

'See his eyelids fluttering? You can make him interested if you just slowly wake him up. He's got to have this colostrum.' Stacking the rustling pillows behind Michelle's head and sitting back to watch.

There's stuff like condensed milk that the midwives reach over to squeeze confidently from her breasts. She can't believe it. Two days ago she would have been mortified that any stranger was touching her like that, but now, after going through the birth, this minor manhandling just doesn't bother her anymore. Let them poke and probe and pump her — she couldn't care less. It's like this big loose body, slack and sore, belongs to someone else.

Her baby's face looks squashed and red, startling in its strangeness. The photo on the baby-oil bottle looks more like what Michelle had expected to give birth to: a chubby little baby with bright rosy cheeks clapping its hands together, a cute wisp of hair curled up on top. When Des had taken a look at his son, that first afternoon, he'd seemed perplexed. The same startled, faintly incredulous look she'd seen on his face when she'd turned and glimpsed him during the labour.

'Do you want to hold him?' Michelle had said, trying to manoeuvre herself up in bed a bit. She was getting good at holding him, not so scared. The way they wrapped him, it was like holding a big parcel of hot chips. Jason's face peered out of the cotton blankets; a tiny old man exhausted after a long and arduous journey.

'Nah,' Des had said. 'That's alright.' He'd wiped his hands nervously down his jeans — a gesture that had almost made her feel sorry for him again. 'How about I go and get a disposable camera?' It was the closest he'd come to apologising for taking hers down to Cash Converters.

'No,' she'd said, stroking Jason's fingers. 'I'll sort something out.' Deliberately not looking at Des, already wanting him to go.

In the middle of the night, when she hears the midwives go down the hall to the nursery or their staffroom, she levers herself off the bed quietly and takes Jason out of the plastic crib even though they've expressly instructed her not to, and lays him in bed with her, wriggling back down beside him. The light in the hospital is cold, and everything hums. Michelle hates the way her narrow bed crackles, the plastic lining inside her pillow that keeps her awake when she knows she should be trying to sleep. She's not tired now, though. She's burning with bright energy, like someone's flicked a light switch on.

'You've got little hands, I've got big hands, let's put our hands together,' she sings to him in a whisper. She invents heaps of songs, in the middle of the night, songs that definitely sound as good as The Wiggles. She lies curled with her tiny oblivious son, hearing his moth breaths, singing softly to him until she has to put him back in the crib before the midwife does her rounds again. They've tried to be strict about it, but she bets they wouldn't push their luck if she told them to mind their own business.

Her wakefulness seems tinged, now, with a private, freshly minted exhilaration.

'Any milk yet?' the staff keep asking her the next morning as they stride in and out of her room. 'Your milk come in yet?'

'Not yet,' she says.

'Keep at it, won't you? Because it stimulates your pituitary gland to release the oxytocin. That's the let-down reflex.'

'Right.' She nods, chewing her lip. If only that nice one would come back, and sit down in her room for a while and explain it properly.

'He's hardly had anything since he was born,' she tells one, worried. 'And he hasn't even woken up properly yet. He won't starve, will he?'

'Well, it's only day two. Just keep going with the colostrum. That's the best thing for him. Just wait another couple of days, and we'll see.'

Jason nuzzles up to her breast, licks it. His tiny mouth feels like a goldfish nibbling at her. Her heart thumps with nervousness.

'Well, that's a start,' says the midwife. 'You have to try to develop his sucking reflex. But there you go, see? He's getting some now.'

Is he? She can't tell what's going on anymore. The girl in the next room, who's up and on her feet and sashaying out to the courtyard for a sneaked cigarette puts her head in Michelle's room on the way back and smiles grimly. She says she's got the opposite problem, her baby feeds too vigorously. That's what the midwives call it, at least.

'He's like a shark,' is how the girl puts it. 'I'm telling you, there's this huge crack in the skin, it's bloody agony.'

Michelle nods sympathetically. She can hear the girl's baby crying at night; the strong, confident wail of an alert child with a big appetite.

'When I get home,' says the girl in a conspiratorial whisper, glancing round before she speaks, 'I'm putting him straight onto formula. I don't care what any of these nipple Nazis say. Stuff this for a joke.'

Michelle sees the poster on the Monday afternoon when they let her briefly get up, and she walks slowly down to the courtyard herself for some fresh air.

$5 FAMILY PORTRAIT. Let a PROFESSIONAL PHOTOGRAPHER do a studio portrait of you both with your new baby. TUESDAYS from 10 a.m.

It's in the mall; just across the main road, really, from the hospital. They could walk there tomorrow, have the photo taken, be back in time to sit up and try the lunchtime feed.

'Do many mothers go and have the family photo taken?' she asks one of the nurses.

'They do, but it's only on Tuesdays, I think,' she answers. 'So you couldn't go until next week. The doctor says you're to stay in bed till Thursday, at least. And you need the rest. But don't worry, they're there every week.'

'I'm fine. I reckon I'm nearly ready to go home.' Even as Michelle speaks, the ache in her is like someone has hooked bricks to her insides and left them to hang suspended. She shifts on her legs as the midwife looks at her sceptically.

'You look a bit pale to me.'

'I'm feeling fine, really. I could go tomorrow.' She feels sweat sliding down her spine, the stitches pulling. Just along the hall and into bed. Then later, after a sleep, they will bring her dinner on that little tray, dessert and everything, and painkillers if she asks for them. And every time she turns her head towards the plastic crib she will feel the same aghast realisation jolting her, the same rush of disbelief, terror and happiness.

'Let Baby find his own way there,' says the midwife when it's time for the next feed, watching Michelle closely as she tries to get the nipple into Jason's mouth. *Baby*. She hates the way they call him that, like he hasn't even got a name. And the way they talk about you as if you weren't there in the room, like the obstetrician who called the trainee midwife over after the birth, when they were weighing and measuring her baby and Michelle was lying there stunned, like a casualty thrown against a wall after a bomb blast, like someone tipped out of a wheelchair.

'There, see that?' he'd said briskly, somewhere down between her legs. 'That's a second-degree tear.' And the two of them had studied her like a bus timetable for a few seconds before he said, 'OK, thread me a needle.'

She'd steeled herself afterwards, during the night, and put her hand down to finally feel the stitches there. Jagged as a barbed-wire fence, just about, the flesh swollen and unrecognisable as her own. Numb on the surface, and a burning ache inside. They keep asking her to sit up in her visitor's chair to feed Jason, but she can't sit up. She can hardly get herself out of the bed without stopping for deep breaths while pulling herself up on the handle thing over the bed.

'What's that … what's that bucket of salt for?' she'd mumbled when they first wheeled her into the recovery room, bloody and trembling, and walked her into the shower cubicle.

'Perineal trauma,' they'd said.

She hadn't understood what they meant at the time but, jeez, she's got a fair idea now.

Michelle continues trying to feed her baby, seeing his mouth open sleepily and keep missing. She wants to cry with frustration but she's scared to. The midwives and nurses are watching her too keenly, trained to keep an eye out for the new mothers who dissolve into weeping.

'Feeling teary?' one had asked her as she watched Michelle tentatively wash Jason in his bath. 'Like it's all a bit overwhelming? Is Baby attaching OK?'

She'd hesitated and answered, 'Well, no. He's only had

that colostrum stuff since he was born, that's the only thing that's worrying me.'

'What about you, though? Got the baby blues?'

'What are they?'

'Well, crying all the time for no reason, say.'

Michelle, concentrating on supporting Jason's fragile head, had glanced over at the midwife. 'No,' she'd said, truthfully. Before the birth, maybe. But not anymore.

The person she'd been before the birth, in fact, seems like a dopey, thickheaded version of who she's become now. So optimistic it was all going to change somehow, with Des at the birth. She'd browse mistily through those cards at the newsagent that showed guys with their shirts off holding little vulnerable babies, expressions of adoration on their faces; guys who looked like models, but still. All the time she was pregnant, she thought that that adoration would kick in once Des saw the baby and she saw Des with the baby. She'd had some vague idea that she'd be able to rest and Des would take over and look after them both, hold his son unashamedly in the crook of his arm like the men on the cards.

When labour began and she'd been admitted into hospital, he'd started off being just like he always was, and she'd been so glad he was there at first, just his usual familiar self in the strange room. She'd sensed him pacing around restlessly, grabbing the remote control beside the bed to surf through the channels on the TV up on the wall as she kneeled on the bed, nodding and shaking her head to the midwives' questions. But once the surf of real pain began rolling in, once she started moaning and swearing when people spoke to her, she'd sensed him, in her peripheral vision, getting jumpy. She'd glanced over at him and seen him caught out, with that expression of startled distaste. God knows what she'd hoped he'd do — rub her back like on the video in the antenatal class, maybe, or sponge her forehead with a face washer; she couldn't put her finger on what she'd expected, but whatever it was, this wasn't it. Not this wordless hanging back like it was all beyond him, folding and unfolding his arms. Not switching off the TV just when things were starting to get really rough, and going to get himself a drink.

They kept telling her to listen to her body, which was embarrassing, like doing those neck massages at the antenatal classes. But in a rush, to her distant, pinpointed surprise, she realised they were right. It was like something she'd known once and then forgotten. She just needed a minute or two to gather her strength, unhook the heavy monitoring belt from around her belly, get off the bed and kneel on the floor. Grab one of those towels. Then she'd know exactly what to do.

But they'd started reading the slip of paper that was spooling out of the monitoring machine like a long, slow shopping docket, and more people were hurrying into the room with a trolley and fitting together forceps like giant soup spoons, and it all happened too quickly at the end, after all that work and going so slowly, and Des wasn't even next to her when she turned her head to look for him.

When they handed her Jason, though, it was like she finally stopped thinking about Des. Stopped worrying about him. She leaned over and smelled her son's head, fresh as newly turned earth, then glanced over at her boyfriend, who was back now, bashing an empty Gatorade bottle mindlessly against his thigh and jiggling his leg in his stretched tracksuit pants as he sprawled in the chair in the corner, so freaked out he couldn't even meet her eye. *Useless*, she'd thought, feeling a startling surge of impatient, adrenaline-fuelled scorn. She was suddenly way beyond him now. She couldn't believe she'd ever needed him for anything.

You find one thing, then you piece together another thing, thinks Michelle in the blue-lit middle of the night, holding her son in the bed. Des has never been the type to let her in on what was happening, kept big segments of his life closed off from her, and she's remembering how someone showed up at the door for him eight weeks ago with a court summons, and how afterwards he'd just banged back inside and sat down again in front of the TV.

She thinks now about how she just sat there with her mouth shut and how guilty and nervous she'd felt checking his wallet for the piece of paper later, to find out what the charge was.

Aggravated assault. She recalled the night it must have happened: Des coming home and wrapping up his bleeding hand rather than go down to Casualty to get stitches, muttering about how it had only been an after-footy argument at the pub.

If it had been his first offence, it might have been different, but she's not stupid. He's got three priors for similar offences and that means no more probations.

He's said nothing to her about it. Not a thing. Even though the court date is this Thursday, and even though he's got a girlfriend with a newborn baby. That'll be the first thing he'll mention, though, you can bet on that. He'll get his solicitor to stand up there and use her and Jason to try and duck the sentence. But no more probations means he'll go straight to the jail from court. Not a word to her. It's like he thinks that if he ignores it it's all going to go away.

Michelle strokes Jason's ear, flat and perfect against his head. First one thing, and then another thing, and the click when it happens, like a door opening. When none of her own clothes had fitted her four weeks ago and she felt so bloated and huge, she'd pulled on one of Des's shirts over her stretched t-shirt. Out doing the shopping, she'd had to fill up the car, and stooping there uncomfortably at the bowser, trying not to breathe in the petrol fumes, she'd come across a folded-up supermarket docket in the breast pocket of the shirt, a discount petrol voucher at the bottom.

As she was waiting in the queue to pay for the gas, she'd glanced at the list of items on the docket, idly working out the computerised abbreviations for Pepsi and peanut butter. *TEABGS50PACK*, she read. *BBQDIP250GRAM*. Then, a little further down the list her eyes took in: *CNDOMS8PACK*.

Her hand swam out and clutched the counter, and the baby seemed to somersault inside her.

'Steady on, love!' the man behind the counter called jovially when he saw her face. 'You're not going to have it here, are you?'

The thing she couldn't get over, after she got back in the car and sat staring at the steering wheel and feeling the baby settling again, was that she remembered that night too, the way he'd bought those chips and dip to take home to his eight-months-pregnant girlfriend, then gone out alone. And how she'd believed he'd been thoughtful that night, buying snacks and renting her those DVDs to shut her up and keep her fat and dumb and happy. Thoughtful.

'You have to come in tomorrow morning, alright?' she says to him on Monday night. 'At 9.30. We're taking Jason to have our photo taken.'

'What day are you allowed home?'

'Maybe Thursday.' She waits, watches to see how

he'll handle this. Pushes him. 'Did you get that capsule from the council like I asked you? Otherwise we're not allowed to put him in the car.'

'Yeah, I know.' There is a long pause. He scratches the back of his head, then his hand moves around to his jaw. 'I've got this court thing in the morning on Thursday.' He mutters it from behind his hand.

Jesus, does he think she doesn't get what's going to happen?

'You'll have to get your mum to come and get us then, won't you?'

'You reckon?' His face is a flinching mess of blotchy discomfort.

'You'll have to put the capsule in her car,' she says, gritted and deliberate, eyeing him, 'and get her to pick us up.'

When Michelle had first met Des's parents, they'd been sitting in the backyard having a barbeque, Des and his younger brother Kyle slouched in the deckchairs while his mum ran around bringing them food and cans of beer.

'Look at your jeans,' she'd clucked at Des. 'White paint all over them. What have they got you doing down there at the centre?'

As if he was working on a real job, not a community service order.

'Painting the lines on the basketball courts,' Des answered, and his father had given an explosive laugh, coughing through his mouthful of beer and chips.

'Not a bad wicket, eh?' he'd said after they'd finished laughing, shaking his head with something like admiration. 'Not a bad gig, instead of doing the time.' And he'd leaned over to Michelle. 'You'll have to watch this one, love,' he said, smiling. 'He can be a bit of a naughty boy.'

She'd smiled back at the time, she remembers. Felt herself as indulgent and forgiving and tolerant as his mother, like it was a club women belonged to. Staring at Des now, Michelle thinks that's exactly what he looks like: a naughty boy. She pauses to make him look at her, refusing to smile.

'Or you could come in and get us, Des, after the *court thing*, and take us home.'

'Well,' he gulps, caught out, 'it's all gunna depend, you know —'

Michelle cuts him off. 'That's why it has to be tomorrow,' she says. She hears Jason sighing in his sleep in the crib.

Des gets up without arguing, and she feels the power that comes with coldness.

'Bring something for the baby to wear,' she adds flatly as he goes to leave. 'Buy something. I want him to look really good.'

She knows the doctor will say no if she asks him, so when he comes on his rounds the next morning, she just doesn't ask.

'Milk come in yet?' says the midwife who helps her

bath and wrap Jason, and she shakes her head with a bright smile.

'Is he sucking, though?'

'Oh, yeah, he's starting to.' Nodding until the midwife writes it down on her card and goes out.

By the time Des comes in, the two Panadols she's saved from last night are waiting with a glass of water and she's all showered and ready.

Des hands her a big bag, grinning. Inside, wrapped in a plastic sleeve, is a miniature leather motocross jacket, covered in outsized zips and logos. He stands there with that idiot chimp smile on his face, and for a few seconds she thinks she might punch him square across the mouth. Her money, her baby allowance, already gone into their joint account. A hundred dollars easy, it must have cost, when she hasn't even got a change table. She touches the cumbersome collar, imagines it chafing at Jason's soft neck. She pulls at her own shirt, which is itching and straining across her chest. Her boobs feel like two watermelons stuffed down her front. She should have bought a bigger size, she thinks, wincing as she pulls a cardigan over the top.

'He'll be a little bikie,' says Des.

God, how could she ever have thought he was good-looking?

'Yeah, but he'll grow out of it in a month,' she mutters.

He's not listening, of course. He's already unwrapping the baby, awkwardly wriggling his arm out of the cotton cloth to work the jacket onto him. Michelle wants to bat his hands away. She banishes the thought of Jason ever lying naked in the crook of Des's arm and methodically swallows the painkillers down, one after the other, to give them time to take effect before she has to walk across to the mall. Jason might grow out of it, she thinks, but Des never will, and there's nothing she can do about that now. *The let-down reflex*, she thinks fleetingly as she holds out her arms to take her son. Let-down is right. The story of her life: numb on the outside, and a burning ache inside.

'You're not really going for that photo?' says the midwife disbelievingly at the desk when they walk past, wheeling the new pram.

'Yes, we are,' says Michelle. 'I'll be back at lunchtime.'

Let them give her those doubtful looks. Jason, in his doll-sized leather jacket, is tucked under the Winnie-the-Pooh rug; Des is with her and on time and with a decent shirt on; and now she's up and walking and the tablets are actually kicking in, she feels like she could keep going all day.

It's all set up at the front of the indoor supermarket complex when they get there: a corner like a stage set with lights waiting for a play to happen. Bales of hay, a wheelbarrow full of flowerpots, a pile of stuffed toys and dress-ups for older kids, props that look familiar to her from dozens of similar photos she's seen that contain them. The photographer's sitting waiting in a canvas chair, sipping on a takeaway coffee and reading the paper.

$12 Kids portraits, says a sign. *$12 Passport photos.* *SPECIAL: $5 FAMILY.*

'What are you after?' the photographer says idly.

'The five-dollar family,' says Michelle. 'The portrait.'

He gets up straight away at the tone in her voice, folding his paper with a snap. She can hear it too, the new hint of steel there.

She checks her face in a mirror, applies some blusher and brushes her hair out, then checks again. That'll have to do. The stitches are killing her and she eases herself gingerly onto the chair, sitting them the way she's planned it: Jason on her lap, Des with his arm around her. Dragging pain makes her face damp with perspiration; it's like a flush of heat goes through her, a tensed fist tightening.

'Just like this, please,' she says, and the photographer leans into his viewfinder and holds up his hand.

As the flash goes off she blinks involuntarily, worried she'll look stunned in the photo when she needs to be alert and smiling, needs one image at least that looks right.

'That's great,' says the photographer, 'especially because your little man there just opened his eyes.'

'Did he?' says Michelle, looking down at Jason. A tiny frown creases his curved red forehead, and she cups her hand around his head. *I pushed this head through my body,* she thinks distantly, marvelling, feeling the fragile bones.

'Wait then,' she says hastily, 'one without the jacket.' She tugs the thing gently off the baby's arms and throws it behind a hay bale.

'Look up, and we're there,' says the photographer. 'All three of you looking at the camera.'

Michelle can feel it — this will be the one she'll choose. She'll put it in a frame, up on the shelf next to the cards and miniature teddies. Make some copies for her aunties. The feeling sealed, at least, like evidence; a feeling that appears out of nowhere, thick and sweet and full of mysterious antibodies.

The second flash makes the room swim and shimmer. And Jason, poor little sleepy Jason lying crookedly on her lap, jerks backwards flailing his arms and legs, and she feels the surprising, determined strength in his sudden kick.

The startle reflex, she thinks, the name dropping into her head from somewhere. Her baby gasps and his eyes widen in astonishment at the world he's woken up into, and he opens his kitten mouth. A wail pierces the air around them, a cry sharp as glass.

It sends her scrabbling ineffectually with her one free hand to pull her cardigan over her chest to hide her shirt, the spreading dark marks appearing there, the shocking flood of sodden warmth.

Milk. Unbelievable. It's as if the cry is pulling a wire through her, all the way up from the stitches. Her whole body bends to him, held tautly suspended by that wire, pulled forward by it, mesmerised.

'What are you *doing*?' hisses Des, jumping up. 'You're outside *Coles*.'

But his voice is like someone you're hanging up on, going small and high-pitched and distant as you put the phone down. It doesn't matter anyway. She's got everything this baby needs, now. And he's twisting his head, searching for her. He knows it too. She puts her hand to the side of his face and looks finally into his eyes — blue, like hers — and his say *it's you* and hers say *yeah, it's me*. Then her hand goes to her shirt, hurrying to get those buttons undone and out of the way.

Some women describe the let-down reflex as a tightening or tingling sensation, the brochure had said. It's not, though — not for her. It's like a shiver rippling out of your control; the way tears will start when something makes you forget, for a minute, what you're supposed to be holding them back for.

Cross-Country

It's the language that gets you. The way it tells you you're through a portal, just when a portal, a doorway — something, anything — is exactly what you're groping around in the dark for. And the idea of links: such a sly touch, coming at the precise time you feel that every link in your life is sundered, every piece of the chain snapped apart. Links are what you're after; linked hands, connections, answers, the web like a big stretched safety net. So you point and click. After all, you've got all the time in the world now.

Peeled. That's how you feel, when it happens. Flayed. People who tell you to get out and move on, they're standing there in a thick layer of skin, cushioned and comfortable, brimming with their easy clichés like something off a desk calendar. *What doesn't kill you makes you stronger. Living well is the best revenge. You were too good for him anyway.* There's a queue of their text messages on my phone. *Call anytime,* they say, *if you need to talk.*

I don't know about you, but I don't need to talk. I need someone else to talk. I need answers. I wrap myself in the spare-room quilt, and watch the screen verify my password and let me in. Like a bouncer, taking pity on me, eyes sweeping my try-hard clothes and unclicking the rope barrier with nothing but disdain.

Live in the world, and there'll be a trail you leave behind you, even if it's a trail of crumbs. That's what they call them, don't they? Cookies. No matter how vigilantly you try to cover your tracks, they'll be there. The recorded minutes of a meeting you attended, some team you've been on; there's your name on the screen. Try it for yourself and see. Google your name, in one of these extended empty sessions of free time when the cursor's waiting like a foot tapping, and there's nothing else in the universe you can think of that you need to find out about. There you suddenly are, undertaking all the trivial pathetic things you think are hidden, so that anyone in the world can see you exposed.

My workmates ring me and pretend I'm on some kind of sabbatical or planned holiday, assure me that all I need is a nice long rest. Rest — here alongside the looted stack of cookbooks and the depleted pile of unwanted, rejected CDs.

It takes a special kind of thoroughness, a particular grim determination to sever all ties, for him to redirect even his superannuation statements and subscriptions to his new address. Even the mail he would have thrown away immediately never arrives now, suggesting that he'd do anything rather than leave a single excuse for re-contact.

So I am reduced to this: typing in his name. A man of forty-two, a successful man with a wide circle of friends and acquaintances, a man armed, let's face it, with the cream of the recipe books, kitchen utensils, bed linen (*I've only taken what I'm sure is mine*) and CDs he's picked through, a man unable to disguise the excess of his baggage — that man shouldn't be hard to locate. It's not as if I'm going to go over there, drive past his house, lie on his lawn drunk and make a scene, harass him. It's just a few shreds of information I want. I supported him for a year, after all; surely I have a right to know whether he's finally submitted that thesis and where, incidentally, the graduation ceremony is to be held. If he's joined a church group or a golf club, I need to paste that into my new identikit. I'll take any crumb, any trail, any vague lead.

What I really want is a chatroom. Under the cloak of the spare-room quilt, all I would do is eavesdrop, just for the sound of his voice. Well, not the sound, of course, but the cadence. Ideas expressed without that clipped and guarded reservation he abruptly adopted: *I think it's pointless considering mediation at this stage. I think it would be best to make a clean break. I think it's clear to both of us it's not working.*

It's 2.30 in the morning when I enter the portal, stoop to the keyhole and whisper the name that turns the deadlock.

I don't know why they call it surfing. They should call it drowning.

Down through the layers of US family-tree pages and rambling travel blogs of dull strangers, I hit paydirt at last. My heart knocks in my chest. I find he's attended a conference, but not presented a paper there. Thesis still unfinished, then. Too many emotional upheavals. His thoughts too scattered after a traumatic breakup, distracted by guilt and second thoughts. I'm settling into this train of thinking, hungry for its possibilities, as I spoon up the dregs of the instant noodles from my styrofoam cup, grimacing at the taste of polystyrene that permeates them no matter what sachet of pseudo-flavour you sprinkle in.

I could of course tip this dehydrated space food into a real mug before I pour on the boiling water, but that suggests a familiarity with habitual loneliness that even I draw the line at.

See, this is the difference. Your partner dies, and everyone comes over with casseroles; they clean your house and hang out your washing. Your partner leaves, though, and you don't need nurturing, apparently; you need avoiding. Your washing grows mouldy in the machine, your friends who told you that what doesn't kill you makes you stronger look at you uneasily, taking in your greasy hair and unwashed pyjamas, and leave you to go back to bed at 5 p.m. Impossible to explain to them the humming, welcoming warmth of the screen later, the peaceful blue light, the endless possibility of an explanation that would make sense.

There's the full name, match sixteen of about three thousand red herrings. He's on some kind of roster. *Show cached text only*. A roster for a sporting club. Not interstate, then. Just the other side of the city, probably. One of those beachside suburbs he always said he'd like to live in. The banner across the top of the page shows that it's a cross-country running club.

I sit back in the quilt in my chair, staring at that page. Obviously no time for the doctorate. Not when he's decided it's time for some social contact, time perhaps to get fit, to shed academia a little, to make some new friends who don't know the disastrous details of the last few months. I picture him struggling up a hill, panting, grateful for the after-parties and barbeques, the light-hearted neutral banter of friendly competition. Or maybe punishing himself, pushing himself to physical exhaustion so that he can sleep nights. Running from something —

that's it. Can't he see the symbolism?

It's ten past four. Jittery with caffeine and MSG, I snoop in the desk drawer Google has no qualms about throwing open for me. He's way down the ladder: coming thirty-fourth. That must be humbling. Thirty-fourth in a field of what — fifty or so? That would make anyone feel like a nameless nobody in a crowd, a face blurry in the back of someone else's photo, reduced to nothing but pixels.

'See, you can reduce all this to just a system of binaries,' I remember him explaining when he showed me how the computer was programmed. 'Just infinite combinations of zero and one.' I wonder if he understands that better now, struggling home in the middle of the pack. How it feels to be rendered, finally, to those low-resolution dots of shadow and light, a conglomeration made up of nothing and one.

'Getting fit how?' demands Julie from work when she rings. 'Volleyball? Aerobics?'

No, I tell her, I need something bigger, more of a challenge. I'm just going to start out with light jogging, then join some kind of club. Some kind of running club.

'Running? Are you serious?'

'Sure. I'm going out today to buy the shoes.'

There's a short film looping in my head and, in it, I'm pounding easily along over a hilltop in an interclub event. I'm not even puffing as I overtake him, despite the spurt he puts on. He glances sideways; he sees it's me. I flash him a surprised-yet-calm smile of recognition, a flutter of the fingers, and pull away. Later, at the picnic, I'll turn when he approaches, and let that awkward moment stretch out. In some versions, I have a little trouble placing him, so that there's the slightest hesitation before I say his name. Then I ask him how his thesis is going, and watch his face fall.

Any day now, I think as I lie heavy as a stone under the quilt, I'll go out and buy those shoes.

From the thin stack of discarded CDs, I pull out the country-and-western collection a girl group sold us one night at the pub. They were great, those girls. Big hair and pointy boots and, up close, plenty of in-your-face eyeliner and juicy-fruit lipstick as they laughed and signed my CD. He hadn't liked them, though. Didn't like the venue (too smoky), didn't like the audience (nobody there to converse with about Thesis), didn't even feel comfortable ordering a couple of beers at the bar. All twitchy about the two guys playing pool, the ones who might have even had a dance with me or at least found it in themselves to relax and enjoy some live music.

'You're not playing that Tammy Wynette Hormone Band again, are you?' he'd say when he came out of the study, irritable and peaky, mind on higher things. 'Jesus, it's like three cats being strangled.'

I put them on now and hear that mandolin, their harmonies start up. *The high lonesome sound*, they'd called it in the song's intro, as I'd smiled apologetically at the guys at the pool table while one of them held out a cue to me and raised his eyebrows, that smile never leaving his face. I'd shaken my head. High lonesome, and high and dry, standing there with a guy who checked his watch every three minutes and coughed pointedly all the way home.

Oh, I'm too far gone, they sing now through the speakers as I turn up the treble and fiddle with the volume. *I know I've loved you too much for too long, but I'm too far gone.*

Take care, Rebecca, they'd written on the CD cover when I'd handed over my twenty bucks, *and enjoy!* Take care — that's good advice. Like all the revelatory news I've received over the last three months, all the bombshells — *I'm leaving*, say, or the doctor's blunt, *You're depressed* — it comes in a handy two-word dispatch, so there's no excuse for not paying attention.

What are they doing now, those girls, I wonder. Not surfing the web all night eating two-minute noodles in a pair of stretched tracksuit pants, I'll bet. When they'd sung those words, they'd sounded sincerely sorrowful, but their cowboy hats and red fingernails had said otherwise. They'll be fast asleep, ready to rise late and meet each other for breakfast at a street cafe, wearing sunglasses, wondering whether to have the hash browns or the bacon.

All I need to do is get up, wash my hair and dress and go to the mall to buy the shoes, and I can get started. I need that torso tight as a rubber band, my number tied and flapping across my chest, my shapely arms working like pistons as I make him eat my dust. That's the main thing.

What do you actually do in a cross-country run? I have a hazy picture of splashing across streams and jumping fallen logs, slogging up muddy hillsides and crashing down the other side through rugged bush. Climbing racks of tyres bound together with rope. No, wait — that's the army. Do you follow a system of flags, or does someone give you a map? Do they start you off with the crack of a gunshot, abrupt as a slap in the face or the slamming of a door?

I wonder too if there's a back-up vehicle, some support staff who tail-gun the runners, just in case you fall into a puddle or a ditch and lie there overwhelmed with the pointlessness of it all, the ludicrous challenge you've imposed on yourself; your foolish, desperate need for purpose. I imagine being lifted from the dirt by kind hands, and given a bottle of Gatorade and a sympathetic pat on the shoulder. Oh, I would give in without even a pretence of fighting spirit if someone offered to drive me to the finish line. Who wouldn't?

I'm shaken from this reverie by a phone call from my boss, ringing me to remind me that my sick leave has run out and I need to return to work the following Monday. Until now I've let his calls go through to the answering machine. This time I finally lift the receiver.

'How are the stress levels?' he says. All casual. 'Getting plenty of sleep?'

'I was dozing when you rang, actually.'

'Good on you. That sounds like just what the doctor ordered.'

No. What the doctor ordered is still an unfilled prescription in my wallet as I self-medicate with net-surfing and the Tammy Wynette Hormone Band. I wander into the study as he talks, my fingers absently, lovingly, grazing the keyboard of the computer. Double-click on the internet icon, go straight to the club site. Last week's results are posted, and there he is, placed forty-second now. A nagging cold, maybe. Slipping down the ladder into numb mediocrity, driving back to his new beachside apartment to sit slumped on the new Ikea sofa and wonder bleakly whether he should open a couple of those cardboard boxes, pull out the old photos from where he's hidden them, and then, and then ... swallow his pride to pick up the phone. He'll ring late, sheepish and sad, voice thick with tears. Ask me if I feel like some Thai takeaway, or just a bottle of wine. If we could talk. It seems so possible, so likely, I feel my throat tighten in anticipation.

'Rebecca? Hello?' My boss is still on the line.

'I'm here,' I say. 'Monday morning, then.'

'We're all looking forward to having you back.'

'I'll bring in something for morning tea,' I say.

So what I'm going to do, I'm thinking, since I have every right to, nothing to do with him, is ring the club and ask about joining. I'm looking for a phone number I can try, and I refresh the screen and start again.

It's amazing, isn't it, the level to which we'll invent what we need. I'm actually expecting that phone call, the high lonesome sound I'm certain will come, from a man beaten into remorse and resignation after a day's cross-country running.

I've convinced myself of it, despite knowing that he hated sport so much — it's coming back to me now — that he couldn't even bring himself to pick up a cricket bat at a family barbeque in all the time we were together. Couldn't jump up and have a good-natured hit, couldn't have a simple game of pool, couldn't bear ever doing anything he wasn't an expert at. The portal opens, and his name is listed again, his beloved, lost, unique name, but I suddenly notice that this list is headed by a title I've somehow missed on the cached page.

Just two small words again, going off in a blinding flash like a grenade. What they say is: *Under-fourteens*.

I sit staring at them, dully open-mouthed. It's like being doused with a sheet of muddy water, like a final jarring stumble on wrenched ankles. I take in a gulped breath at the sensation of some huge gaping distance being covered, a long stretch of terrain rushed through with a whiplash jerk, and then, as it all skids to a halt, my face cools as if raised to a merciful and unexpected breeze.

Click on the icon, close the screen. *Windows is shutting down*. I almost hear it, the decisive thud as it hits some imagined sill somewhere. I need a shower, and then I need a long cold drink of something at an outdoor table, but first I linger, watching the innocuous sky-blue screen. I'm waiting for the little melody it always plays before it sighs and switches itself off, that melancholy minor-key tune that tells you that whatever you've been watching, ready or not, it's time to roll the credits.

Sleepers

Ray was stuck in traffic, an unusual feeling in a town the size of his, inching forward through a detour round the railway crossing. He watched the orange text changing on the roadside electronic billboard in the lethargic kind of trance he'd felt himself lapsing into more and more recently. *TRACK UPGRADE*, he read. *DELAYS EXPECTED. DETOUR AHEAD.*

He'd forgotten — they all had. Barrelled up to the intersection into town as usual to find the contractors had been hard at it from 6 a.m. just as they'd promised, a squadron of shining earthmovers and excavators hacking away already. Thousands of dollars being spent every minute by whatever construction company had won the tender. Not anyone local, that's for sure. Ray might have had some contract work himself, then.

Up ahead, a guy in reflector sunnies, fluoro vest and

hard hat was propped next to a *STOP/SLOW* sign.

'That's gotta be the easiest money in the world,' Ray's girlfriend Sharon had said to him once in the car as they waited at some roadworks. Ex-girlfriend. Having a dig at him, Ray had thought, because he'd done a stint himself on a road crew the summer before.

'Not always,' he'd answered, knowing it wouldn't do any good, but weighing in anyway. 'Some motorists, they just get out of the car and king-hit you, because they're sick of waiting. Two blokes have been run over deliberately, just holding signs like that.'

She'd given him a look. 'That'd be why you get the extra loading, is it? Danger money?'

'Go ahead and laugh,' Ray had said with a shrug, releasing the clutch. They'd been on their way to his sister's for a barbeque, he remembered, and looking at her he'd suddenly felt the same deep dragging inertia he felt now. The sight of her there, holding a cling-wrapped pavlova in the passenger seat, mouth a sour twist, her pink blusher sparkling in a shaft of sunlight. Something creeping over him like a slow anaesthetic.

'I've tried,' she'd said a few months later when she told him they were splitting up, 'but it's all going downhill.'

'I thought we were going good,' he had answered, hearing the whine in his voice, hating it, 'and now you're telling me you're moving out.'

She'd rolled her eyes like he was the thickest kid in

the class. 'Not me, Ray,' she'd said. 'You. You're the one moving out.'

SLOW, the sign said. And then the flashing arrow for the detour, down past the boarded-up hotel and the old saleyards. Ray yawned. He'd be late, but everyone would be late today and, anyway, the manager was never out the back, at the warehouse where Ray worked three days a week, and lucky to have that. So what if he was late? How many nested imitation terracotta pots could the public want in one morning? He idled, watching the traffic, exhaust fumes shimmering in the dust raised by the labouring machines on the line, their battered metal teeth jerking and tugging at the railway tracks, trashing them.

SLOW. SLOW. STOP. Then flip, his turn.

The road worker aimed his mirrored and shadowed gaze at Ray as he drove past and gave a wave that had been reduced to its bare minimum: a single, slow-motion finger lifted in acknowledgement that here was one man passing another man who was pretending to be doing a job of work, bored shitless and leaning on a one-word sign. Ray raised a finger off the wheel in response, glancing at the expressionless face and looking away again. Didn't know him.

Up ahead he heard a splintering crack, like ice, as an excavator levered up one of the railway sleepers, the big engine surging to get purchase on the gravel.

By late afternoon, when Ray was at the pub, there was already talk of the sleepers.

'They're pushing them into piles,' Frank was saying. 'Sorting them from shit to good. So they've got to be selling them on.'

'See, if that contractor was a local,' said Vince, 'anyone could go and help themselves to some of them for firewood. Anyone at all.'

'Not these bastards. They'll be selling them on to some other subcontractor, any money. That's why they've got that barrier round them. They tender for these jobs and they screw the last cent out of 'em. That's the way they do business.' Frank, who hadn't worked for fourteen months.

Afterwards when Ray drove Vince home down past the intersection, he saw the old sleepers piled high — big dark timbers, rooted up now and useless. A string of flapping orange flags erected around them.

'If that's the barrier,' Ray said, 'it looks fairly token.'

'Thing is,' said Vince, pointing, 'people'll be after those for landscaping. You wait. And they'll go to the other spot they're working on, that old crossing out of town.'

'They're pulling all that up too?'

'Mate, they're pulling up five k's of line — there's gunna be millions of the things. Tons of 'em. This company'll never notice a few disappearing. You wait.'

Ray nodded. He'd seen gardens himself, of course,

edged with old redgum sleepers. It was just the kind of thing Sharon had always been on his back to do, landscaping the garden.

'Why do it,' he'd argued, 'when we're just renting?'

'Ray,' she'd said, exhaling a breath of resigned frustration. He'd waited for an answer, but she'd only repeated it as she'd turned away. 'Ray, Ray, Ray.' Almost tenderly.

And him standing there, stranded, never knowing what she was going to want next.

'Redgum,' Vince was saying now. 'Beautiful. Burns like bloody briquettes. You watch this town — winter coming on and a pile of scrap wood like that. A little string of orange flags isn't gunna stop anyone.'

The sleepers — those perfectly good redgum sleepers and a sudden professed desire to landscape — it was all Ray seemed to hear about over the next two weeks. Bernie at the warehouse told Ray, with a kind of defiant righteousness, that he'd grabbed a ute-load late at night to finish off his pool area. Someone at the pub achieved fame by liberating thirty sleepers in broad daylight with two mates, avoiding suspicion by donning fluorescent vests to do the job.

'And that's fair enough,' Bernie said, slapping price stickers onto a shipment of outdoor furniture. 'You can tell by the way those piles are graded that whoever's got the tender is just going to put a match to the crap ones.'

'I guess,' said Ray. Inside the opaque layers of shrink-wrapped plastic on the pallet, he could see stacked ornamental Buddha statues. It was like gazing into a submerged shipwreck, crammed full of calmly waiting monks.

'I reckon get in now, and get what you need,' said Bernie. 'Just do it discreetly, and don't take the new replacement stacks. Don't get greedy.'

Ray lifted his knife and sliced through plastic, breathing in the chemical, sealed breath of some factory floor in China. He thought of waking up that morning with an empty plate from last night still sitting on his chest, gently rising and falling, his hand keeping it steady, in exactly the same position he was when he'd fallen asleep. A white plate, round and innocuous as a moon.

At Steve's barbeque that night, he walked up and down the brand-new paved barbeque area, bordered by lines of sleepers. Set at intervals in the freshly shovelled topsoil were small clumps of perennials, which reminded Ray somehow of a hair transplant.

'It looks great,' he called, feeling Steve's eyes on him.

There must have been something wrong with him, some bug he had — how else to explain that bottomed-out energy, the sapped, exhausted feeling as he watched Steve turning steaks on the grill? He'd go and have a check-up. A blood test.

'A rustic border,' Steve was saying. Full of focus and

purpose, pressing here and there on the meat with the tongs. 'That's going to grow in no time.'

Ray swatted a mosquito in the dusk, racking his brain for something to respond with. Nothing.

'We'll have a pool in here next,' Steve added. 'Get rid of the lawn altogether. Just an outdoor entertainment area. You right there, Ray?'

'Yeah, good.'

'You wanna grab yourself some coleslaw?'

'Thanks.' He hoisted himself up from the chair, putting down his warm beer. Another thing: these last couple of months, he'd felt this heavy squeezing under his sternum, slowing him down. Shouldn't have worn shorts. Should cut down on the beer. He walked over to the trestle feeling the eyes of women on him; Steve's wife, Sue, smiling over, other wives and girlfriends raising their heads to glance at him, going back to their wine. The only single man there, he realised, feeling something speculative in their glances, something indulgent.

He'd driven past Sharon's house tonight and seen a car in the drive he didn't recognise. He couldn't stop thinking about it; his brain was like a dog jerking on the end of its chain over and over, returning to it. So that'd be the thing to do — get chatting to someone else, let word get back to Sharon that he was out there, available, a catch, on his feet. But even though he could feel those eyes on him (*car in her drive*, that convulsive choke in his throat as he circled it again), he sat back down with his laden plate on one of the sleepers instead, because the thought of trying to get a conversation going with any of them felt like heavy lifting. And they knew all about him anyway; a 35-year-old man who lived in a Colorbond shed at a mate's place, not exactly unemployed but a part-time storeman. A liability, not a catch.

'Just temporary,' he'd said when he first moved in to the shed, 'just till I find a place of my own.' Back then he couldn't imagine spending winter in it, holed up there with only the shed heater, the cold coming up through the cement floor. And how gradually it had happened, putting a piece of carpet down, buying the lounge suite at Vinnies that time, putting up the TV aerial. Telling himself he was saving money. Finding his feet. Waiting for things to go from shit to good.

'Hey, Ray,' a voice was calling him. Steve's teenage son. Scott. Sam. Something.

'Come and check this out,' the boy said, beckoning Ray over to a big black telescope on a tripod, pointed straight up into the night sky.

'Not quite dark enough yet, Sean,' Steve called from the grill, scooping meat and sausages up onto a platter. 'Wait till it's dark and I'll show you how to adjust it properly.'

Ray stooped and squinted through the lens.

'I think it's Mars,' said Sean.

The smell of him — grass and sunscreen, sweat and energy, all of it barely contained — registered in Ray's head with a sudden painful awareness. This shortness of breath, the pressure on his chest … He thought of his old man's heart attack, the way he'd staggered crabwise across the lounge room, his arm out, wordless. Take him five weeks to get a doctor's appointment, anyway. He'd ring tomorrow.

'Is that focused now?'

'Yeah, that's good,' answered Ray. He could make out a blur, a jittery nebula like a reflected car headlight, then blinked and saw something else there in the lens, something dilating, sweeping closed and open again. His own huge eye reflected; the lid creased, a maze of lines spreading like rivulets.

'Is it Mars?' Sean said doubtfully.

He'd taken the boy out fishing one time, he remembered, with Steve; clowned around pretending to fight a carp he'd landed on the bank. Casting all day, that day, into snags. He blinked again, saw the pouched skin around his eye wrinkle like crumpled old paper, his own pupil staring at him black as space. If he had a son now, he thought, he'd be fifty when the boy was fifteen. So probably all for the best, then. He let out a breath that hurt like a stitch.

'Yep, that's Mars,' he said.

Turning the keys in the ignition in his car, he fought the impulse to go home via the house again, check if the car was still there. Up his old street, the same streetlight broken, up to the driveway that he used to pull in to every night, taking that normalcy for granted. His ute bumping up over the kerb and the sensor light snapping on as Ray got out of the car in his loser shorts, running to flab, any fool could see that. Then Sharon's silhouette in the ridged glass of the front door, her and whoever was there with her. He saw her put both her hands up to the glass to peer through its distorting ripples at him.

Don't worry, he heard her saying, her voice muffled, *it's just Ray*, seeing him for exactly what he was; he could hear that in her tone. Her right arm lifted and snapped off the sensor light impatiently, leaving him there in the dark, and the shapes of the two of them rippled and shifted as they stepped back from the door, Ray thinking he would never forget this one moment as their shadows swam together out of the light.

He opened his eyes and saw he was still sitting in his ute outside Steve's place, his hands slack on the steering wheel. He tried to tally up the beers he'd had. Tried to send a message down to the deep-sunk part of him, scudding along somewhere, to kickstart itself again.

He had an idea — a half-arsed idea, he berated himself, a crap idea — to head over to the crossing and put down the tailgate and load in a few sleepers. Twelve, maybe. Enough to take around tomorrow to Sharon's place. His mind swerved over this bit — the dropping them unannounced onto her front lawn — and went straight to the moment when he'd be lowering them squarely and surely into place between some solidly hammered pickets. And her surprised gratified smile, lost for words for once, as he went away and came back with a load of topsoil from Jenner's and spaded it in. Her instant landscaped garden, ready for some seedlings.

He could manage loading them up himself, he was sure, if he raised one end first then pushed them onto the tray. Or get a mate. Get Vince to help him. He checked his watch: 12.40. Vince would be snoring in front of *Rage* by now, three bongs down.

It was when Ray got down to the track and saw the motionless machinery there, the dark mountains of sleepers silhouetted, that he felt his original idea begin to melt and solidify into something else. Why should he do a damn thing for Sharon? Hanging round her place like a whipped dog. Why shouldn't he score some for himself? Take them home, cut them up with the chainsaw, make a decent firewood stack. He imagined, briefly, the shed heater radiant with cosy warmth, stoked with redgum, glowing all night. Or — and this was better — why shouldn't he keep some whole, do some landscaping for himself, build up a couple of beds and plant some veggies out at the shed?

Ray realised he was at the crossing, sitting motionless again in the cabin, staring at the flattened earth where the railway track into town used to be. All of it scraped as bare as something strip-mined now. A plan dropped onto the town from above, not a single local employed. You could understand the ire, the harmless, face-saving looting of all this wood pushed into unwanted piles. And he was so tired of this, the way he kept finding himself hunched over, eyes closed like he was hibernating, the way he had to rouse himself to move.

Ray stretched as he stood, his spine cracking. In the back he found himself a pair of gloves, let down the tailgate, and here came the moon, sailing out from behind a cloud, ready to help him. Sean, if he was still up, would be able to see every crater on that surface, it was so clear. Ray ducked under the orange flags and tugged at a sleeper, pushed and pulled it free, dragged it over to the ute and heaved it in with a grunt. Easy. Another one. Another. He'd only need ten. Some people he knew had taken dozens of the things. It felt good, even though it was the middle of the night, to be working up a sweat. Cold oxygen in his lungs prickling like stars, clearing his fogged head finally.

What could you grow in winter? Potatoes, maybe. Beans.

Ray was considering the pile, wondering which piece to haul free next, when bright blue lights rolled across it. A lazy roll, rhythmic and silent.

He'd been humming; hadn't heard the cop car pull up.

And as he turned, squinting in their sudden high-beam, his chest squeezing, all that false warmth descending into his boots, he knew that they wouldn't bother with their siren, because they could see that it was just him. Just Ray. They knew he'd turn around like this, and take what was coming to him. Because they need an example, he thought wearily as he peeled off his gloves, the realisation flaring like a little chunk of burning rock, a tiny meteor.

What was the word? An escape-goat? Nowhere to put the gloves, so Ray threw them onto the ute tray, and missed. The cops' headlights casting big crooked shadows.

He waited there for them, next to the sleepers, lowering his bare hands for comfort onto weathered, solid old redgum, hauled up and discarded but with so much life in it, still, it just broke your heart to see it go to waste.

Whirlpool

'Mum says you better get inside right now.'

Your sister, Louise, is already getting ready for the photo: she has one big hot-roller pinned to the top of her head and two small ones at each side, and she's applied the skin-tinted Clearasil to the faint outbreaks on her forehead and chin. The cream is not the colour of skin but the strange pink-orange of a bandaid, or a doll.

'She says you have to come right now or you're going to be in big trouble.'

Louise's ridiculous hair-roller, like a poodle's flopping topknot, makes you less afraid. She sighs with irritation, hands on hips, and her shadow throws a long shape across the surface of the pool like the elongated silhouette of your father in all the family snapshots, stretched across the foreground of the lawn as he takes a tentative photo of you and Louise on either side of your mother, in front of the rosebushes in the sunshine.

Two weeks ago, shuffling through these photographs for something to send out with her Christmas cards, your mother tossed the whole stack irritably down onto the coffee table. 'I really have to get something professional done. Something decent. I can't send one of these — every one's a disaster. We're always stuck there squinting straight into the sun.'

You all waited, silent, braced for the rest.

'There isn't a single shot,' she added with finality, 'where we don't all look dreadful.'

And you thought, *all*, seeing your mother centred there in the pictures, gripping her two girls, your father nowhere — just a peripheral shadowy shape, stretched thin.

Louise stalks back inside as you splash defiantly from one side of the pool to the other in two languid backstrokes. You want to stay in until you are bleached, until your fingertips turn white and wrinkled, then lay yourself down on a towel to soak up the heat from the cement path, thinking of nothing. You float suspended, sun through your eyelids a brilliant red, telling yourself that any minute now, you'll heave yourself out. You'll surrender this lightness.

*

Summer begins the day your father carries the armfuls of aqua plastic and piping out from where he stores them in the garage and mows the yard before rolling out the heavy plastic-coated base that will become the pool. Heat rises from the ground, cicadas pulse in one long thumping vibration. Sometime, in the second week of December, he brings home a Christmas tree from the stall run by the scouts outside the shopping centre. When he hauled this year's tree inside, your mother gazed at it in long-suffering disbelief, her arms folded, and when he went out again for wire to secure it, she crouched in front of it with the box of decorations, glancing at you and Louise with a conspiratorial smile.

'Do you think,' she whispered, widening her eyes comically, 'that they keep the dud one specially for him, every year?'

You made yourself smile, complicit, and then, as she watched, the two of you draped the tree dutifully with the balls and bells. Even when she left the room, you still worked silently and rapidly, like it was homework, winding tinsel over the outsized branches, ignoring each other.

Your mother spends the hot summer days inside, watching tennis on TV, occasionally raising her frosted glass of iced coffee delicately to her temple. In the corner the fan turns its head back and forth, stirring the thick air.

'My God, you could set your clock by him,' she says and sighs, looking out the window to where your father is sweeping stray leaves off the pool surface with a net.

You hover there clenched, rooted to the spot.

'It's bad enough we haven't even got a proper in-ground one and you girls have to put up with that stupid thing that should have been thrown out years ago,' she adds. She turns to you then, extending her arm to take you in, watching you. 'He's absolutely obsessed, isn't he?'

You feel yourself nod and smile again; a sickly, traitorous smile of concurrence.

Your mother squeezes your shoulder and says, 'Would you like an iced coffee too? It's so hot, isn't it?'

On the TV screen someone slams the ball down the court and there is a ripple of applause. The fan shakes its head slowly at you, silent and censorious, and you take a hasty swallow of your iced coffee, loaded with ice-cream, so sugary it hurts your teeth.

'I suppose we'll have those next-door kids round with their towels first chance they get,' your mother says, her eyes restlessly tracking the ball across the court. 'God knows their parents wouldn't think to plan anything for them for the school holidays. Just expect me to feed and entertain them.'

Each morning of the school holidays, you feel a faint, smothered panic that the pool will sooner or later be the subject of attack. You try to stay casually offhand as you change into your bathers and escape out the back door. You can feel Louise doing the same, picking up her folded towel with studied nonchalance, as if the thought has just occurred to her. You slip through the house, expressionless and furtive, avoiding your mother on the way out.

'We'll have those kids from next door traipsing through the house for a swim every day now,' your mother keeps saying to your father, but Leanne and Chris never come in through the front door anymore. They stand hopefully by the fence in their own baked-dry square of backyard with their faded bath towels, waiting to be invited.

'Climb over,' you whisper to them, glimpsing them through the palings, piling some bricks against the fence for them to step on as they scramble down.

With other kids there, you and Louise break your pattern of avoidance, and four's better for playing Whirlpool. You all run around the sides of the pool, your legs threshing the water, stirring up a slow, slopping current. After you build up a strong whirlpool, you take it in turns to tumble into the middle and be spun around, outstretched. Chris doesn't like it and the rest of you have to wrestle him sideways to throw him in. You feel a surge of sly, teeth-gritted pleasure at his protests, his skinny, weak-limbed acquiescence. You watch the helpless ridge of his spine arching as he flounders, gasping, and your power is cool and blue and chemical. He has to learn. You girls eye each other, expressionless, as he staggers humbly to his feet afterwards, blinking and choking. Then you grab the sides and start running again for the next turn, feeling the water resist and drag against your thighs.

Out there in the centre of the vortex, when it's your turn, you close your eyes and you can feel the current flexing like a muscle. You open your eyes and you're in the middle of it, letting yourself be loose and helpless, staring up at the aching blue of the sky. If you could rise into that sky you would see everything spread out far below: the neat rectangles of backyards and tiled roofs, and dotted here and there, little round pools of aqua chlorinated water, like bright precious stones, full of light. Yellow grass around the edges, where water has slopped out, as kids played Whirlpool.

*

Back inside the house, it's dim and airless, thick with the piney, December smell of the Christmas tree in the lounge room.

Your mother comes clicking across the lino in her beautiful yellow linen dress.

'It's about time,' she says. 'We're having the Christmas photo done today, remember?' Her voice is bright, her lipsticked mouth curves into an animated smile. You can tell by her tone that the photographer must already be there. In a whisper she adds, as you turn to run, 'Ten minutes. Get yourself down here looking presentable. I mean it.'

Louise is in the bedroom you share, standing at her half of the dressing table and running a tube of bubblegum lipgloss over her lips. Her hair is looped stiffly back at the top with a rainbow comb and two tendrils curl at the front of each ear.

Your heart sinks at what's lying ready for you on the bed. 'The sundresses?'

'That's what she said.'

Louise has hers on already. She's thin, so it doesn't look quite so ridiculous, but yours is tight under the arms, where it's elasticised, then sack-like all the way down to mid-calf.

'She said you have to wear your sandals too,' Louise adds.

You peel off your damp bathers and pull the dress on, tugging it over your chest. You try to brush your hair up and into a ponytail like Louise's, but it's too long and lank, and without your mother's hairspray and tail comb it just looks flat and lopsided. You're sunburned too. You're going to be bright pink in the Christmas photo.

The dress is squeezed across the tingling, embarrassing swell of your chest, a nine-year-old's dress. A few weeks ago, you'd tentatively said you wanted a training bra for Christmas.

'Oh, *darling*,' your mother replied, looking at you indulgently. 'You're barely twelve, you're nowhere near old enough for that.' Her tenderness felt as treacherous and irresistible as a tide, something you leaned into, hypnotised, as it tugged you off your feet.

'*Anna*,' your mother smiled kindly, her voice low, 'it's

normal for young girls to feel self-conscious about their weight, sweetie.'

And you saw Louise's triumphant smirk. She's giving you the same sneer in the mirror now as you pull down the dress.

'It's just as well you have to wear a dress like a tent, anyway,' she says airily, arranging the curling wisps of her hair, 'because you're so *fat*.'

The breath falters in your throat; hidden, mastered.

The photographer's presence charges the atmosphere as your mother lets her voice carry lightly from the kitchen, apologising for taking up his time, offering him a cool drink.

As you come in she's pausing to arrange a vase of roses on the mantelpiece next to the row of cards lined up upon it. They're all from the friends she writes to every year, in Canada and England — friends she's faithfully kept in annual contact with since they all met fourteen years ago, when she and your father went on their honeymoon cruise to Tahiti. Their cards are decorated with frosty holly and robins, sometimes crusted with glittery bells, and the ones from Canada often contain a printed page-long letter that begins: *Dear friends!* That's part of December's smell too: the scent of these cards, cool as snow, the English ones which say things like, *Gosh, hasn't the year flown?* and *Christmas greetings to your two little girls there 'down-under'!*

At the beginning of each December she sits at the dining-room table writing, a stack of blank cards and a list next to her. 'One day,' she says to you, 'you'll thank me for keeping up all these contacts for you; you'll be able to stay with all these people when you go overseas.' Her own unsent cards are ready now — each completed in her neat hand, stacked in their unsealed envelopes on the table. Each waiting for a copy of the family photo.

Your father's there, sitting on one of the armchairs in a fresh shirt.

'Wait,' says your mother, and you all listen, ready to be prompted, the photographer with his eyebrows raised enquiringly. She pauses. 'Can you get the Christmas tree in the background too? You see, it's for our Christmas card — we have a lot of friends overseas.' She turns sunnily to your father. 'We met them while we were on the cruise, didn't we, darling?'

That word in your mother's mouth, the way she looks your father in the face to say it, her touch on his arm as she goes past, makes something turn over in your stomach, cold and glassy. You shudder. You can't help it.

'Sure,' says the photographer, moving his tripod.

Your mother adjusts a basket of white-sprayed pine cones on the occasional table next to the couch. 'Do you think that looks Christmassy, Louise?'

'Yes, Mum.'

'Well, put that little angel holding the candle there too, will you, darling?'

You have dawdled, you have spent an illicit five extra minutes in the pool after being summoned, so Louise is the favourite this afternoon. You can feel it in the way your mother's hand drops onto your shoulders, the pressure that pushes you down, which says, *Just you wait.*

'You sit there,' she directs, steering you, 'in front of the couch, on the floor. And, Louise, you'll be on this side of me and, Robert, you on the other.'

Your mother checks her hair in the oval mirror over the mantelpiece, and sits down.

'I think we're all ready,' she says now to the photographer, raising her chin. Her long elegant legs are tucked sideways.

Next year, you think, the friends will write: *You haven't changed a bit!*

You're all touching and it feels weird. There's your mother's knee behind you, encased in nylon, which must be so hot today. And next to it, your father's lanky shin. You feel it press against you — once, twice, as he shifts and leans forward.

'I put the hose in the pool for you,' he says in a low voice. 'We'll let it fill up a bit more, eh? So it's all ready.'

Your mother hears. 'Robert, do you think we could forget about that dinky little pool just for five short minutes?' Her voice is almost breathless with forced breeziness.

You stare at the eye of the camera lens looking blankly back at you, lined up on the couch for display.

'Try to keep your eyes open and your mouth closed, Robert,' your mother says with a little trill of laughter, and you think suddenly, with dull, hopeless bitterness, *He's never going to answer.*

'Everybody smiling!' says the photographer.

You know the kind of smile your mother will be wearing: radiant, triumphant, the teeth just showing. The way your father will be sitting straight-backed and uncomfortable, in the frame for once. You glance across at Louise.

It only takes a second, but you're stunned to see her, at the exact same moment, looking back at you. Something passes between you. It's like the reckless moment after running hard around the pool's perimeter, when you eye one another, savage and panting, before launching Chris or yourselves into the stirring, threshing current of the whirlpool.

Then you both turn back to the camera, and you do not smile. You know Louise is doing it too; keeping her face compliant and empty. The camera snaps like teeth.

'Another one, eh?' says the photographer. 'Big smiles now, girls.'

You let another dead, robot smile turn up the corners of your mouth. With your eyes you will your mother's friends to understand, to walk to the window and tilt the photo into the English or Canadian light, frowning, seeing everything encoded there. They will see how stiffly you are sitting in this humiliating dress, cross-legged like a child, how heavy and proprietorial your mother's hand is on your shoulder. They will imagine the weight of that hand. You understand, as the camera's indifferent shutter clicks again, that the sundresses are about your mother, that what you'd seen in her face when you'd asked for the training bra was a tremor of terror, not scorn. All this blooms in you, too fast, the flash's nebula blinding as phosphorus.

'OK then,' says the photographer.

'Can we go now?' you hear Louise say, and you feel a thrill of fear at the sullen flatness she dares to let her voice betray. She can take this risk because the photographer is there, humming; an oblivious circuit-breaker. The photos are inside his camera now, inviolable.

'Course you can,' your father says before your mother can speak. 'Too hot to be inside on a day like this, trussed up in your best clothes.'

He'll pay for that, that *trussed*. You think of him picking up the towels abandoned on the path and hanging them on the clothesline each night at dusk. The final solicitous, regretful sweep of his hand he gives them before he turns to come inside. Heat is rising in you.

'Maybe just a couple of portrait shots of the two of you,' the photographer is saying to your parents.

You witness the opposing forces of charm and chill collide in your mother as she's caught off guard. She hesitates, then says hurriedly, 'Yes, yes, of course,' and there it is, you're sure of it now; you glimpse in that moment her wire-tight thoughts running ahead, grim with the need to plot exile and allegiance, the constant undertow shift of churned, compliant water.

You run upstairs to yank the dress over your head and pull your still-damp bathers back on, tugging pins and clips from your hair as you go.

Then you're out the screen door, running headlong towards the turquoise-blue, brimming full now, cool and shadowed, like a watching eye about to overspill with glinting, unshed tears.

Cake

She's sitting in the car outside Kidz Rezort. All she has to do, she tells herself, is put the key in the ignition, and turn it. Fire up the car and drive away, like all these other mothers. Liz sits there helpless, though, unable to move, watching them surreptitiously as they walk away from Kidz Rezort and, God, she hates that spelling, that Childcare R Us branding bullshit, that voluntary illiteracy. They're so *breezy*, the other mothers. Chatting, some of them, or taking out their phones to check the next thing on their schedule for the day ahead. Holding a latte, or holding a phone, but none of them holding a child's hand, all of them divested of toddlers and seemingly glad of it. And they might look preoccupied, but not guilty. Nobody looks guilty, do they? Nobody else is eating themselves alive like this, trying not to run to that childproof gate and tear back in there, scoop up their kid from the floor of the Tadpole Room and run screaming out of the place.

Liz knows that if she did that now, if she was to give in and leap out of the car and hurry back up the path, that would be the end of it. She'd spot Daniel through those soundproof double-glazed doors of the under-twos room; doors designed to prevent the noise escaping, the telltale roars and wails of inconsolable, bereft toddlers scanning the room desperately for their parents. She'd see him red-faced and beside himself, or hunched miserable and bewildered in a corner with a plastic toy shoved into his hand. She'd see the professionally patient faces of the childcare workers glance up at her with expressions that say *you again?* and *look, we're busy, can't you pull yourself together?* They're nice enough, the staff — God knows she's quizzed them at length — but there's no denying they're harried. They have to spread themselves thin. And he's in there, alone, where she's left him. Abandoned him to a roomful of rampaging strangers: big, chunky, runny-nosed buzz-cut boys in miniature camouflage gear, already seasoned commanders of the play equipment and the puzzles. Not that there's going to be anybody with enough time to notice that Daniel needs help to get up onto the swing, in any case. But still. It's guerilla warfare, that's why they call it a jungle gym, that's why those boys are dressed like mini commandos. That's where she's leaving her baby.

You can get yourself theoretically ready for this, Liz thinks, you can do all the abstract peripherals — name on the waiting list months ago, three sessions of accompanied play to get him used to the place — but there is still this moment, of holding the car keys after you've left your child in there, your breath squeezing and ragged so that soon you'll have to re-apply the eye make-up you put on so carefully this morning for your first day back at work.

She won't return until five. Eight hours. That's a long time for an eighteen-month-old baby. Isn't it? Even though he's not the youngest in there, not by a long shot. That's what they've been telling her, repeatedly, like that's supposed to make her feel better, instead of worse.

She digs in her bag for her lipstick, her fingers searching for the small cylinder, and pulls out a crayon, then a battery, then a tampon, then a gluestick. Well, stuff it: let her workmates see her just like this — blotchy and thin-lipped, blouse and skirt not quite fitting her the way they used to. But she can't arrive too late, not on her very first day back.

So she sets the betrayal in motion, starts the car numbly and finds reverse, lifts her foot from the clutch and pulls away from Kidz Rezort. Around her in the swirl of peak-hour traffic, she sees other drivers gesticulate as they talk into their hands-free mobiles, or else stare straight ahead through their sunglasses. All of them, she thinks wonderingly, have probably dropped off their children for the day; all of them have put it behind them and are *functioning*.

She's one of them now: out of the baby pool, free and unencumbered and alone, heading off to work. Earning. She punches 'play' decisively on the CD player and wonders if she's the only one on the road who's singing about driving in a big red car.

Another set of glass doors: her own boundary gates this time, back at her old office, still with the two dusty ficus trees in the foyer, unchanged; perhaps they're plastic, she's never noticed before. Her work colleagues all at the same desks, Stella at the front reception, same smell of cardboard and carpet vacuum powder; only the calendar has been changed. Tim and Dave and Julie all wave enthusiastically to her as she walks with Caroline down towards her old cubicle as Stella calls, 'Hey, everyone, look who's back in the land of the living!'

'Here you are,' says Caroline as they arrive at the desk, and Liz, struggling with monumental time-warp, almost turns to see if she is in fact there, sitting in her tweedy ergonomic chair: her old self, pre-baby, looking up enquiringly, slimmer and with a better haircut.

There's a pause before Caroline adds, 'Well, sit down, then!'

She does, quickly and obediently. The smell of the place, that's what throws her, the scent of it all, adult perfumes, air breathed out by computers and printers and photocopiers. Plastic and paper and cold coffee in the plunger, over there on the bench. Dry-cleaned jackets and cool, processed climate control. She fills her lungs with it. What's he doing, right at this moment? Howling? What's it been, an hour and a quarter?

Liz blinks, concentrates on the surface of her desk, all tidied up ready for her; she can see the faint streak marks of the sponge, smell the residual Windex. Whoever's sat here in her place for nineteen months has obviously liked pot plants — there's a couple of dead ones left on the windowsill. Same computer, same shiny worn spot on the space bar, measuring out a million incremental small spaces.

Caroline's still hovering over her desk, though, clearly expecting conversation. She's changed her hairstyle. It's red now, and spiky.

'So, how old's the little fella?' she says.

'Eighteen months last Tuesday,' Liz answers.

'Ohhh! Is he really cute?'

'He sure is.'

Caroline props her hip against the edge of the desk. 'Got any photos?'

'Yeah, I've got a couple here, I'll just …' She unloads her mobile phone from her bag, her diary, some pages of notes to herself, and finally the compact red photo album she's brought so she can show everyone at once.

'Are they photos?' calls Stella, beaming as she comes over. Now Julie. The women flip through the pictures, exclaiming over her son.

'Look at him here in this one, on the swing!' they say.

'Here he is swimming!'

'He can't actually swim yet,' says Liz. 'He's just in the baby class.'

'That curly hair! He's *so* adorable!' cries Julie, squeezing her eyes shut.

Liz glances up across the desks and sees something pass between Tim and Dave — an eye-roll, a resigned grin. Then the faintest headshake, unmistakable to her. Disdain.

'I bet you've been counting the days!' Julie goes on. 'When I had Toby, I couldn't wait to get my brain working again after all those months home bored out of my skull.'

'Oh God, yes!' says Stella, ever competitive. 'You forget, girls, when I had my kids there wasn't any of this coming back to work. You were just stuck there, getting driven up the wall.'

'It just sneaks up on you, doesn't it?' says Julie. 'Baby brain. Head turned to mush.'

'Yep,' says Caroline, 'it's the monotony that gets to people, they reckon.' She closes the photo album with a sigh and gives it back to Liz. 'I mean, it's wonderful and everything, but the day comes when you just want to get your own life back, right?'

They've all said their piece and now have turned to look at her expectantly. Liz can't remember the last time she's had three adults waiting on an answer from her like this. It's not something you'd think you'd ever lose the knack for.

'Yeah,' she blurts. Yeah, yeah, yeah, they're right, of course they are. Here she is after all back in the land of the living, ready to make jokes about midnight feeds and daytime television and projectile vomit, ready to roll her eyes and give a dismissive headshake, a theatrical shudder.

'I mean, with mine,' Stella says, watching her hopefully, 'it was honestly like someone had thrown a grenade into the house. I mean, your marriage is never the same. It's just very, very hard to adjust. Isn't it, Liz?'

No smiles now. Now it's the we're-here-to-listen faces, still and avid for meltdown details.

She feels a jolt, a strong kick, of defensiveness. Like a power surge. 'Actually,' she says, 'I've quite enjoyed it.'

There's some alliance that wavers and falls at her words: she can feel it as their eyebrows go up in surprise.

'Well, that's good,' says Julie at last, flatly.

'I mean,' she fumbles, feeling her face flush, 'I'm very glad to be back, of course, but I actually *like* staying home. I've liked it, I mean.' She senses, as they nod and smile, that this is not the answer they want.

The three of them return reluctantly to their own desks and for the next hour, as she starts scanning the backlog of spreadsheets on her computer that will bring her up to date, she senses a card being secretly circulated around the desks. There will be a cake, she thinks, at morning tea. That's the way it's always gone. Cake from the supermarket, in the end, because Tim and Dave complained once that they were outclassed when it was their turn to make one, and it was fairer to just buy one. So it will be lamington fingers, drowning in sticky, sugary coconut; or a shining chocolate mud cake on a plastic plate; or a fluffy block cake with orange icing crumbling like a sandcastle. These are the cakes that have marked each office birthday and celebration, cakes that leave a fur of sugar on your teeth and a pile of brightly coloured crumbs, cakes you need to empty the remains of into your desk bin when nobody's looking.

But she's mistaken. At midmorning, as her colleagues mill with coffee mugs around her desk to present her with the card inside an office envelope, smiling and joking, Julie clears her throat. Card, but no cake. Some momentous new development to announce.

'We've got a new office policy, Liz, to have birthday and welcome-back cakes on the first Wednesday of each month,' Julie begins. 'We were just having cakes all the time. Too many celebrations; we had to cut it down.'

'Right,' says Liz automatically. 'Good idea.'

'So because we just had a farewell cake this month for Sandy who was doing your job, we'll have a cake for you Wednesday fortnight, OK?'

Liz picks at the envelope flap self-consciously. 'You don't need to get a cake.'

'No, we will, because it'll be for Dave's birthday too and you can share.'

The card is a tall cartoon bird wearing a sheepish smile and holding a suitcase under its wing. *Welcome back!* says the caption inside, surrounded by signatures.

'I thought that was appropriate,' says Stella, tapping the card, 'since it's a stork, and you've been on maternity leave.'

Tim sips his herbal tea, and Liz instantly remembers his sacrosanct ceramic jar of special imported teabags in the kitchen. 'That's not a stork,' he says. 'It's a spoonbill.'

Tim hasn't changed an iota in eighteen months. How could she have forgotten this need for constant, ridiculous, social smiling?

'You should see the photos of Liz's little boy,' says Julie, ignoring him. 'Danny.'

'Daniel,' mutters Liz, but they don't hear her.

'You remember we've got that meeting this afternoon, don't you?' says her boss, Frank. 'Sorry to throw you in the deep end, but that's what got scheduled.' He grins. 'See, got to crack the whip now. Got to get you back into gear again.'

'No problem,' she says.

Once they leave her cubicle, she phones Kidz Rezort.

'I'm just wondering if he's settling in OK,' she says, keeping her voice down.

'He's fine,' says the reassuring voice at the other end. 'He's riding a scooter across the play area right now.'

'That's great. Just checking,' she says. Swallowing down the desire to spit: *Do you think I'm an idiot? He's eighteen months old. He can't even balance on a fucking tricycle yet. You're looking at the wrong kid, you negligent morons.*

'Thanks for that,' she says in a cheerful inane sing-song. Got to keep them happy with her, got to have them onside. She hangs up and rests her fingers again over the keyboard, hearing her breath going in and out, in and out, staring at the glowing screen. *Delete*, she presses. Punching the key like a bird pecking. *Delete, delete, delete*.

There's a pamphlet in her bag called *Returning to work after maternity leave*. She picked it up at the Infant and Child Welfare Centre and knows it off by heart, especially the front page.

A woman, younger than her, lifting a laughing baby into the air. No bra-strap showing through her shirt, no midriff bulge. Shiny hair.

Being a stay-at-home mum can begin to seem mundane and repetitive to many women who have experienced the challenges of a satisfying job and the stimulation of daily adult conversation, it begins.

Baby brain, Julie had called it, the clichéd term, the enemy hormones, the surprise attack to halve your IQ. Actually Julie's coming towards her now, threading her way down the aisle between the desks, carrying another orange envelope. More spreadsheets maybe, thinks Liz. But Julie holds the envelope up and smiles.

'Hope this doesn't seem rude,' she starts, 'but can you put in three dollars? For the morning tea.'

'For the …'

'The once-a-month morning tea. For next month. See,

we started out taking it in turns to make a cake, then some people said they were too short of time to do that and started buying cakes.'

'Yes, yes, I remember. I was here.'

'Oh, right, sorry. Anyway, once we'd started with that, it didn't seem fair that some people were taking the time to make them at home and not others, so we decided we should all just buy them and we'd all put in three dollars a month so it was equal.'

'Sure, yep. Here you go.' Liz fishes out her wallet and finds a five-dollar note, snaps it shut before she has to look at the photo of Daniel tucked in there. His shy smile like a boobytrap. He'd have his thumb in his mouth right now. Not smiling, that's for sure.

'I'll just get you your change,' says Julie.

'Please, don't worry about it.'

'No, no, look, it's right here in the envelope.'

God, these endless extended moments where you're left in limbo, the time dangling like a suspended toy on a piece of elastic. She'd forgotten. She's been taken in by a stupid pamphlet. She holds out her hand for the coin, unable to keep her feet from jiggling with impatience. Julie folds back the envelope flap and stands there, still hovering.

'OK, so what sort do you want?' she asks.

'What sort?' Liz blinks.

'I'm buying it next month, from Cake It Away, and you can have carrot or hummingbird or chocolate mud.'

Liz stares at Julie's plump mouth working. Her mind's a desperate blank, scrabbling to summon a response. Baby brain. It must be.

'Um … I don't mind, Julie. Whatever you think.'

Julie looks dubious, then her face clears. 'I'll ask Dave.'

She wanders off down between the desks with that leisurely amble they all seem to have. Liz can't remember noticing it before now. All the time in the world, here in the office. Once you're clocked on, it's the calm progression from in-tray to out-tray via the full range of possible distractions. Spin it all out. She has a sudden vision of herself at home, hastily mashing vegetables in the kitchen as Daniel hangs onto her leg, angling herself to keep him away from the oven, picking him up and hauling wet washing out of the machine with one arm, balancing his weight on the crook of her hip. She wants that weight now, God, she craves it, settled firmly into her side; she's unbalanced without it. In fact, her arms hesitating over the keyboard, haphazardly recalling how to set up a mail merge, feel weirdly light and empty. She'll ring Kidz Rezort again. No, no way in the world can she ring them again. Do it. Don't do it. Delete, delete, delete.

There's a manila envelope in her top drawer. She finds it as she's checking in there for some scrap paper, and pulls it out and opens it. Inside, notes in her own handwriting.

It gives her a shock, seeing it there. With sudden clarity she remembers the day she jotted them down — sitting breathless and uncomfortable, eight months pregnant and with a hard insistent baby head pressing down on her pelvis, readying itself — projecting her anxiety into worrying that the person taking over her job wouldn't understand the importance of what she was leaving them with.

Liz looks at her own notes now, underlined here and there for emphasis. *Delete fourth Excel column before printing for subtotal!* they say. *Account for Henderson's must be in triplicate and invoice photocopied!* Underlined, she thinks with amazement. And those conscientious exclamation marks, as if it all urgently mattered. As if it meant something, as if things would fall apart without her, as if anybody could give a flying toss. She might as well have been sitting here, she thinks, with plaits and a school tunic on, so distant and foolish and naive do those exclamation marks seem now.

Rewarding as caring for a baby can be, says her pamphlet, *it is often a relief to exchange it for a return to the paid workforce where your expertise and skills are valued.*

Jesus, now what? It's Stella this time leaning on her desk, smiling like the bearer of wonderful news.

'I hope you didn't bring anything from home,' she says, 'because we're taking you out to lunch!'

Liz remembers the place they take her. There's pokies in the other room and the bistro's got a nine-dollar lunchtime special. It's crowded with other office workers.

Liz is keyed up, berating herself every few minutes for not coming up with a fast excuse for Stella. Her brain has let her down, it's AWOL, it's definitely elsewhere. If she'd pleaded another plausible engagement she could have slipped away, made it back to the childcare centre in her lunch hour and just checked that he was alright. Reminded them that he needed a drink before his sleep, and that he took a while to settle. Then she could have driven back to the office, and nobody would have known. She might have seen him, calmly asleep after all on those bloody gym mats they used for cots, safely cocooned in a blanket. Instead she's here confronting a slab of lasagne oozing bright orange grease, surrounded by white noise, poker-machine din, and Caroline, Julie and Stella. They're being good sports, Liz thinks. They're doing their best, they're being as sisterly as they can. She must try, she really has to. She takes a bite of lasagne and thinks straight away: *those cheats*. She recognises immediately the instant curly lasagne noodles, the cheap bottled pasta sauce with herbs and red wine, and the shredded supermarket mozzarella. At home, on the single income, they've been living on this homebrand stuff.

'I love Italian,' says Caroline. 'How's yours?'

'Delicious,' Liz says.

'I bet it's a long time since you've sat down and had a decent lunch with the girls, isn't it?'

'Yeah. It sure is. Thanks for inviting me.'

She hopes they've remembered to get his own blanket

out of his bag. Her book says the smell of something familiar is comforting. Maybe she could text them. No, can't text them.

'So what cute things is Danny doing now that he's a toddler? Is he talking yet?' asks Caroline.

Liz puts her fork down, swallowing, smiling. 'You know what, he does this great thing,' she begins. 'You know that song? The one that goes: *If you're happy and you know it, clap your hands*? We make up all these different verses — stick out your tongue, stamp your feet, point at the sky — and even though he can't talk he'll do all the actions. He'll have this expression on his face ...'

She finds herself singing a quick snatch of the song, sticking out her tongue, pointing at the sky. They're looking at her, nodding and smiling, but after a couple of lines, their smiles get a little stiff. Even though Liz sees Caroline glance rapidly at people at other tables around them, it's like strings somewhere are jerking her hands into action, and once she's started she can't stop. She gets to *If you're happy and you know it, then you really ought to show it, if you're happy and you know it, clap your hands!* before whatever spell has caught hold of her lets her go, and she can drop her own hands back into her lap, queasy with mortification.

Sneaking a look at the others, she remembers an occasion a few years ago when a new comedian appeared on TV and they all thought he was hysterically funny. For a surprise she'd organised tickets for the four of them to see him live at a local club, only to find that his stage act was almost identical to what they'd already seen him do on TV.

Caroline, Julie and Stella had laughed dutifully enough, but their faces had shown a kind of pained disappointment, something faintly aggrieved. She sees the same expression in their faces at this moment. That's her, now, she realises. Someone they expected to be entertained by, who actually doesn't have any new material after all.

'I weaned him, you know, to come back to work,' she says suddenly. Where had that come from?

'Well,' says Julie, still looking disapproving, 'it's about time, don't you think? A whole year and a half? I had Jake on formula by eight weeks. You've got your own life — they can't be dictating it.'

'Finally managed it just five days ago, really,' Liz adds. At night, at feeding times, Daniel's been looking at her and the bottle in her hand with a baffled uncertainty that stabs at her heart — she can actually feel it, beating swollen and too big for her body, as his hand knocks the bottle away and dives to the collar of her shirt. A terrible, abject longing swamps her now as she thinks of breastfeeding, the two of them lying on the bed, Daniel's hand dreamily stirring the air as she sings, *The wheels on the bus go round and round* …

Dictating what? she thinks, gripping her cutlery. Nobody's been dictating anything.

She looks away from their patient, indulgent smiles

down at her lasagne, cuts off a corner and shoves it in her mouth. *Shut up*, she tells herself savagely.

'Has anyone got a dollar change if I put in ten dollars?' says Stella. 'Because I'm heading back early to build up my flexitime.'

'But you know dessert's included,' says Julie. 'I'm having the lemon cheesecake.'

'What else is there again?' asks Stella.

'Where's the dessert menu gone?' says Caroline.

Liz concentrates on swallowing the claggy paste of cheese and pasta in her mouth. *God in Heaven*, she thinks, forcing it down, *if anyone else mentions fucking cake again today I'm going to burst a blood vessel*. There's a whole afternoon to go, back in the land of the living, stretching before her like an endurance run, something she's been talked into, something that's meant to prove something. *You signed up*, she rebukes herself. *No point aiming this seething fury at anybody but yourself. You and your rampaging, roller-coastering, oestrogen-soaked, mush-brained hormones. Put your phone with its two hundred pictures away, back in your ridiculous cavernous mummy-bag, and agree to orange poppyseed.*

At three o'clock Frank comes to take her to the meeting. They walk down the hall together. Her shoes are hurting. Maybe the ligaments stretching have made her feet a size bigger. She clacks along gingerly, feeling the pinch at each step.

'You're OK, aren't you?' says Frank.

'Sure!'

'I mean, I can sympathise with you. It's a hard adjustment to make.'

She hesitates, remembers Frank has two kids, or is it three? Met his wife once, at the staff Christmas dinner. Evie. Evelyn. Ellen. God, her memory.

'It is, after you've been in one routine,' she agrees gratefully, 'and then you're suddenly shoved into another. I mean, look what we expect!'

He nods. 'That's what I mean. Having to walk into a room full of pretty competitive strangers, all with their own agendas. That's a bit of a tough gauntlet to run, doing it cold like that, getting thrown into the mix.'

Fresh guilt throbs in her like a toothache. She hadn't expected it would be Frank who understood, but no doubt he's dropped his own kids off enough times at childcare and felt the same thing.

'And just leaving him there in that room,' she says, fighting off hot tears, 'shoving him in there and expecting him to cope, when he's just a little baby. That's it. It's hard. Really hard.'

He walks along in silence for a few strides, digesting this.

'Actually,' he says, 'I meant you. This meeting.'

The tears swim in her eyes, hastily detoured. 'Shit, sorry, Frank. I'm a bit … um, preoccupied. I thought you meant my little boy, at childcare.'

'No, I meant ...'

'Yep, I get it. I'm fine, actually.'

'Not nervous?'

'Nope.'

'You're sure you're right?' he says to her as they push open the door.

'Of course.' Keeping her voice crisp and calm. But so rattled she can barely keep nodding and pretending to take notes, contributing nothing. She can't believe how the meeting drags, plodding ponderously through item after laborious item. Nobody in any hurry — it's like they've all been drugged. And when she does get out of here, when she can legitimately be released and grab her bag and keys from her desk, and leave, she will have just sixteen hours before she'll have to be back here again tomorrow, going through the same thing. The day yawning ahead with tiny variations, the endless clock-watching dreariness of it. The salary. Eyes on the salary.

Then finally it's ten to five, and she's walking, in a jerking, limping semi-run, back down the corridor, burning to be gone.

'See you tomorrow,' she calls to Tim as she hurries past.

'It's like you've never been away,' he calls back, which stretches her smile even more thinly across her face, as if her expression has been hammered flatter and flatter, growing flimsier by the second.

He doesn't run over when he sees her. He looks back to the blocks he's lining up in stacks on the carpet.

'He was really good,' one of the workers says cheerfully. 'He ate all his lunch.'

'That's good,' she says. She's fighting a terrible nausea, feeling the sweat in the small of her back. What would she do, if nobody was watching? Shoulder her way over there, snatch him up, crush him in her arms, howl like a she-wolf?

'Thanks,' she adds. 'Thank you. I'm sure you've done a great job.' Clacks over there in her pinching slingbacks, feeling the button in her waistband strain as she crouches beside him to pick him up.

'Let's go, hey?' she whispers. 'Let's go home.' Her mind filled, entirely, with the smell of him and a corrosive wash of built-up tears like acid.

He seems dazed as she carries him out to the car and buckles him in.

'Did you have a great day?' she asks him brightly, still smiling. *Stay positive*, her book had told her. *Positive but firm*. His eyes rest on her as she searches his face for traces of tears. Then he glances away, like this is one more perplexing event in an inexplicable day, his hands clasped tightly around his lidded cup — and that single gesture almost does her in, almost sends her over the edge. *Perspective*, she thinks shakily as she drives. *Be calm.*

The second she's in her own driveway she's running around to his car door, scooping him out of the car seat, back onto her hip, feeling the weight she's been starving for all day. She's too needy and she knows it, wrapping her arms around him as she carries him inside, nuzzling her face into his neck, nudging him into place in the crook of her elbow, her hand spread like a shield at his back. She can't help herself. Then when she reluctantly puts him down and kicks off her shoes as hard as she can into the corner, she can't believe how casually her husband, Andrew, can take him and balance him on his knee as he asks her about her first day back.

'What?' she says, distracted by his offhand nonchalance. How has she never noticed this before?

'I said, how was it? Good to be back?'

She shrugs, mesmerised by the absent-minded kiss he plants on Daniel's head, the way his thoughts can already be shifting, complacently, to other things.

'To tell you the truth,' she says, 'I hated it.'

He grimaces. 'I thought you were really looking forward to it. You said —'

'I know,' she cuts him off.

Every time their bank statement's come in over the last year and a half, they've sat at this table and made a grim assessment of their down-to-the-wire mortgage. She's sick of talking about it and, anyway, she's willing Andrew to stop what he's doing and look, really look, into his son's face, feast his eyes on their boy, breathe him in. She folds her arms tightly together, still twitching with withdrawal. This can't go on, obviously. She's going to have to do this every day, so she'd better pull herself together right now.

Andrew's mobile beeps with a message and she watches, incredulous, as he reaches into his pocket for his iPhone, holding Daniel around the waist as he leans over, completely dispassionate and unruffled. Liz can see what it is, now. Andrew has always left Daniel, and come back to him like this, every day since he was born, just about. For him, this is normal.

He checks the phone's screen as he releases Daniel onto the floor, then puts it away again, glancing at her stiffly folded arms before getting up to go into the kitchen. Once behind the bench, he takes packets of stir-fry vegetables out of a plastic shopping bag and tips them into a bowl. It's his turn to cook and he likes to be doing something if he senses an impending argument, preferably something domestic which makes his position more defensible.

'You said,' he says, ripping open a plastic tray of chicken strips, 'I remember it was you that said we've got to start getting the principal down, not just pay off the interest every month.'

'I know.'

'Because we're just running on the spot, here. Treading water.'

'You think I don't know that?'

He lights the gas under the wok. 'I mean, Jesus, do you think I love every minute of *my* job?'

'I know, I know, I know.'

'You need to give it a few months,' he says, 'at least, to re-adjust.'

'Yep.' She's got to see this from his point of view. That's what he's going to say in a minute, that they're both locked in, that he wouldn't mind a stint staying home himself, just looking after Daniel, but they need the two incomes, there's no way she can deny it, and then she will answer, indignantly, that she's not denying it. Watching his back, she sends him an urgent telepathic message: *Please don't say it*.

'We agreed it was always only going to be a temporary thing, you staying home,' he goes on in a low, reasonable voice, his back still to her. 'Because, you know, we're locked in to this.'

From behind, he's got a slumped look. Someone on a suburban peak-hour train, unfit and round-shouldered. Some stranger. She's got to try harder, she thinks. Be less dogged, put her head down and focus on the wage and the plan. Quell this feeling that threatens to roar silently out of control.

'What's in there?' she says, keeping her voice light, noticing a white paper bag on the bench.

'Surprise to celebrate your first day back,' he says. 'Cake.'

In Daniel's bedroom later, pulling his pyjamas up over each leg, she asks, 'Was it fun today? Ready to go again tomorrow and play with all those blocks?'

Another thing: she's got to lose this inanely cheerful voice. She tries to sit on the bed in her slippery, lined business skirt and then stands up with an irritated click of her tongue, undoes the button and zip and steps out of it. Peels off her tights too. Better. He's on her lap now, leaning his weight into her, as she picks up his bottle and teddy. Then she feels his small hand rest shyly inside her shirt. She's spent weeks distracting him from this gesture, but the uncertainty of it makes her usual soothing speech stop in her throat. No, no, no, she thinks with a sinking, bruised sense of exhaustion. Be consistent. Pull that hand out gently, and explain again, in those fraudulent words recommended by the baby-care book.

Something is tearing inside her, slowly and deliberately, like a perforated seam. And even as she's admonishing herself that giving in will only make things worse tomorrow, her hands are functioning outside her own volition again, unbuttoning her shirt.

There is a slide between the two of them, a sigh, a caving in. She lets herself succumb. Daniel relaxes into her lap, stretching his toes as he starts to nurse, his hand dropping from her collar, the slump of secret relief. She hesitates, then wriggles out of her creased shirt altogether. Skin on skin, that's the cure-all.

She'll put him to bed soon. Just a comfort feed, that's all it is, and a chance to inhale the scent of him again. She won't lie down because if she does, she'll drift off to sleep and then Andrew will know she's broken her vow about the bottle-feeding. So she stays upright, listing slightly, eyes closed as she starts making a mental inventory. Put him down, put on a dressing-gown, back to the dining room, eat dinner then put on a load of washing. And then, finally, find thirty minutes or so to slip into the spare room to do the second thing she's been aching to do all day: log on to the net-banking site and see if she can do some figuring out. Play around with the mortgage recalculator. Check the interest against the principal.

For this moment, in this pocket of breathing space, she lets that tearing sensation go all the way down until it hits inviolable rock bottom; somewhere to push off from, back to the surface. Then she opens her eyes. She's in full command of her hands again now. She eases the left one from the back of Daniel's heavy head, and carefully, expertly, slips off her watch.

White Spirit

The woman artist, Mandy, tells me on the Tuesday they
need another day to finish the clothing in the foreground
of the mural. She's leaning against the table telling me
this, rolling a cigarette. She's got a look I would call
high-maintenance: hair with lots of startling colour, stiff
with gel and arranged to slope here and there, multiple
earrings up her ear, lace-up combat boots. It's a look
designed to suggest she's impoverished yet bohemian and
individualistic, and nobody round here wears anything
like what she's got on. She and her boyfriend, the other
artist, drive in each morning from another part of town, a
suburb where you can get a double-shot latte early in the
morning sitting on an upturned milk crate outside a cafe.

The residents of this estate took a few surreptitious
looks at this pair when they first arrived, and have chosen
to stay out of their way since. We'll have to invite some

in specially, over the next couple of days, for the photo documentation we need. Some casual shots of the artists chatting and interacting with residents, facilitating important interchange. Community ownership. An appreciation of process. It's all there in the grant evaluation forms.

Mandy flips open some of the books she's brought and taps an illustration. It's of a couple of women in Turkey, standing at some festival in regional costumes, the embroidery on their blouses and hats and vests achingly bright.

'That's what we're after,' she says, dragging on her rollie. 'We're focusing on getting that design right. All the details and colours. See the women there?'

She gestures to the mural, where her partner's painting in the figures of three women. They're prominent, next to the four laughing Eritrean children, who are posing with a basketball.

'Should that be a soccer ball?' I say, half to myself.

'Sorry?'

'Should those kids be holding a soccer ball instead? They've actually formed a whole team; they play on the oval on a Sunday afternoon. I think soccer's more their thing.'

I might be wrong. That might be the Somalis. But a furrow of concern appears on her brow.

'Do they? That wasn't in our brief. But we'll change it, don't worry. We'll just paint over the orange and make it black and white.'

'I don't want to put you out, or start telling you how to do your job.'

'Not at all,' she says, grinning. 'That's what we're here for. Cultural appropriateness.' She exhales smoke and calls. 'Jake! The African kids — it's soccer, not basketball.'

He stops painting, stands up and stretches, and frowns at the mural. 'Do you reckon we'll have to change their singlets then?'

They both stand silently for a few moments, considering the image before them.

'Nah,' she says finally. 'Leave the singlets. Nobody'll notice that.'

They'd said in their interview, these two, that meeting the local community was their chief interest in applying for the job. They'd done similar things elsewhere — one at the Koori health centre, one at the credit cooperative, a portfolio of photos from a wall mural at a community market up in Queensland — and they said what kept them doing it was the rich sense of connection you achieved working alongside the very people you were depicting in your mural, and the growing sense of community ownership through collaboration. When they talked about the celebration of diversity, and how excited they were about all the different cultural groups represented on the estate, I'd felt the centre director, on the interview panel beside me, mentally checking boxes.

Now I look in sometimes, on my way to teaching a

class or driving the community bus somewhere, and I don't want to hang around. They don't seem too excited now. There's nobody there but the two of them, with their big paint-splattered tarps and their ghetto-blaster, music echoing round the empty basketball court as the mural gradually takes shape. Even the kids who usually come in here to shoot baskets after school are giving them a wide berth. It makes me uncomfortable, like I've let them down somehow, like it's our process here at the centre that hasn't worked. It's awkward, this silence; tainted with failure that no one wants to claim. We skirt around it, the three of us.

'You'll be finished by Thursday, won't you?' I say. 'Because the opening's on Friday night and we can't change it — there's local councillors coming, and the minister.'

'Yep. It'll be done. We're used to working through the night, aren't we, Jake?'

He nods and grins back — easy-going, unthreatening, pleasant. And yet nobody's come in here and expressed an interest in picking up one of those brushes and helping. Nobody.

I'll have to round up some of the primary kids in my after-school club tomorrow and get them in here. Take the photos then. We can give out some brushes and they can do some background, or something. Grass. Sky. Paint in those skin tones, all those larger-than-life-size arms draped around shoulders. They'll like that. At least,

I hope they will. I hope they won't bounce off the walls with hyperactivity; throwing paint, scrawling their names, going crazy.

I unlock the office to get my bag out and scrabble in it for money to buy material for the women's fabric-painting class. I'm meant to use cash from the kitty, but it's such a business, writing out a request form and waiting round for the admin officer to open the cash box to sign it off. Easier if I just pay for the plain cotton pillowcases and white t-shirts they like to paint. I park outside Spotlight and race in, arriving back at the car just in time to see a parking inspector writing me a ticket.

'Oh, come on, it's only two minutes past.'

'It's a clearway after 4 p.m. just like the sign says.'

'Look, I'm buying stuff for a class. For a group of refugee women.' I hate trotting that out, and in any case technically it's a bit of a white lie now, but this is my money we're talking about, my free time, my goodwill.

He sighs and looks at me.

'See?' I say, showing him the discount pillowslips, the tiny children's t-shirts. 'Please.'

'Get going then,' he says, deleting something on his machine and walking off. Angry with himself for giving in to me.

He'd be a boy off the estate, himself. I bet thirty years ago he came with his parents from Lebanon and grew up on those stairwells and in that glass-strewn park. I bet he could still tell me the number of his flat, if I asked him. The number, the smell, the noise outside, the silent resolution of his parents to get out.

'Thanks!' I call out, but he's already at the next car up the road, already disappearing in a gritty shimmer of peak-hour carbon monoxide.

'What do you think of the mural?' I say to the women later as they bend over their fabric paintings. 'The big picture, in the gym?'

They smile shyly. 'Good.'

'Do you think you'd like to go in and help them, just do a little bit of painting in there?'

I catch their quick, hidden glances of consternation.

'No, no.' They're all smiling hard. 'Is very nice, but no.'

'You don't want to paint, though?'

'With the girl with the … um, this?' Nahir gestures fleetingly to her tongue, where Mandy has a stud, and all the women giggle uncomfortably.

I smile back, and shrug. I thought they'd like it, a mural that showed their community's diversity. We can all reel the numbers off, the workers here, with a sort of proprietary pride: fourteen distinct cultural groups! Nine different languages! We shake our heads in bemusement at the multicultural, multilingual, multi-tasking jobs we've landed in, where every newsletter and flyer has to be in five different translations, where if we're not running to put up the nets for Vietnamese boys' volleyball we're busy setting up the cooking class for the East Timorese mothers' group.

Maybe there wasn't enough consultation, after all. It's hard finding something everyone's happy with. Or maybe the artists' hair and big boots, their thumping music, have scared them off.

'You'll come on Friday, though? To the opening?' I cringe at the eager insistence in my voice.

They smile, confer among themselves in low voices, and nod obligingly at me. 'Yes. We all come.'

'Because, you know, you can wear national costume, if you like. Your traditional dresses? That would be wonderful. The minister would love to see that.'

Their faces grow wary and apologetic with unsayable things. The room is stiff with a charged awkwardness, with languages I can't speak.

'No. But we come.' They go back to their painting, murmuring and sorting through the photocopied pages of designs. I should get a photo of this, I think absently; this pile of embroidery patterns they've all brought from Turkey, Afghanistan and Iraq, all shared around and used as stencils. If I mentioned it to the centre manager, he'd want a photo for our annual general report. Still, at least they're all coming along to the same class, and God knows that took me a while. Maybe one day I'll convince them to share tables.

Here in Australia, the women don't embroider these traditional designs. They paint them straight onto fabric instead, finishing several pillowcases or table napkins in one afternoon. Out in the gym, the mural artists are painstakingly painting their figures in traditional dresses copied from a library book; in here, in the craft room, the real women are outfitted in pastel windcheaters, some of them decorated with flowery borders of quick-drying fabric paint. I heat up the iron and press their pillowcases flat to make the dyes permanent and washable. Steam billows up in my face; the hot, comforting smell of clean, pressed cotton, the same the world over.

Wednesday afternoon, and Mandy and Jake are still not finished. There are a couple of faces still just sketched in at the front, likenesses they're working on from the health centre's photo album of snapshots from last year's barbeque. It's a rainbow of faces now, the mural, a melting pot. A few Anglo faces are placed judiciously next to Laotian and Eritrean, Vietnamese alongside Salvadoran and Iraqi and Aboriginal, all standing 'We Are the World' style with arms round each other, grinning as if the photographer's somehow cracked a joke they all find mutually hilarious, something that in real life would involve several simultaneous translators and a fair whack of fairy dust.

The centre director is thrilled, the minister's going to love it, the artists have a jaunty spring in their step because the mural itself, it must be said, is stunning. It's a multicultural vision to be proud of. Community workers from other centres and other estates are invited to the Friday opening to marvel and envy, and apply for their own grants.

'You look a bit flat,' says Mandy, raising her eyes from the photo album to glance my way.

'No, I'm great. It looks wonderful, it really does.'

'We've left that bit there for the kids to work on this afternoon,' she says, pointing to an empty section of sky.

'OK, good.'

I'll have to choose five or six kids, I'm thinking, bribe them with chocolate not to wreck it, just paint the blue like they're told.

'Someone here to see you in the office,' a colleague tells me, putting her head round the door. The music's off, briefly, and her voice echoes in the big, empty space.

It's a guy in a suit. He steps forward to shake my hand.

'You phoned me,' he says, 'about the anti-graffiti sealant? I'm here from Pro-Guard, just to inspect the wall surface to make sure you purchase the right product.'

'Oh, yes. Well, we want to treat a mural to protect it against graffiti.'

He nods. 'That's a real asset-management issue now. Our products give years of repeat protection, whether you choose the impregnation-style pore-blocking penetrative sealer or something with a sacrificial surface ...'

He keeps going like this until my head is swimming with compounds, polycarbons, two-packs and one-pot formulations. I keep nodding as he inspects the wall in the gym and talks about polysiloxane coatings versus silicone rubber, and finally I say, 'Look, I need something we can apply ourselves which is quick-drying. And if someone graffities it, I want to be able to clean it off without too much fuss.'

'They won't graffiti it,' interjects Mandy, who's listening. She's walking along past each big smiling face, giving each eye a realistic twinkle. 'Nobody will graffiti anything they feel a sense of ownership and inclusion about.'

'Right,' says the sealant salesman, eyeing her briefly before turning back to me. 'Like I said, we're in the business of helping you maintain the value of your asset and protecting it from senseless defacing. So for your requirements, I'd recommend Armour-All.'

'Great!' I respond, mustering a smile. I'm tired now.

'It's a urethane product. You mix in the solvent and apply two coats twelve hours apart; using masks and gloves and adequate ventilation there's no reason why you can't apply it yourself. And it has terrific anti-stick. You can just remove any graffiti with white spirit.'

'Fabulous. We'll take it.'

He says he can deliver it that afternoon and names a price. I nod, totting up the remainder of the grant money in the account. Just enough left over for snacks at the opening, catered for by the Vietnamese social group. Everyone likes spring rolls, as long as we don't make them with pork. We're having bread and dips too, so the Turkish cooking class members don't get their noses out of joint. And maybe I should get the East Timorese to sing something …

'I'll go and get the after-school-club kids,' I tell the artists. 'We've got to get this done by tonight so we can make sure the sealant's dry by Friday afternoon. The Armour-All.'

Jake and Mandy say they'll help me apply it. They're nice people, really. I don't understand why this whole process hasn't worked out like I thought, like I said it would on my grant project description.

It's got to cure properly, the sealant. So we end up applying the second coat at midnight on Thursday, the three of us slapping our fat brushes into the wall corners, wiping up drops with a turps-soaked rag, seeing it go on shiny and slick and impenetrable. I'm light-headed and starry from the fumes, so that the Nick Cave CD they're playing tonight beats in my skull like a racing, roaring pulse.

I've never been here on the estate this late at night. As I splash the sealant on I listen to cars revving and residents shouting, doors slamming, a quick blooping siren as the police pull someone over, the thumping woofers of passing car stereos. And through it all, I hear a babel of voices; every language group we're so proud of, calling and greeting, arguing and yelling, nearly two thousand people I couldn't name and who have no use for me. Who glance at me, leaving in my car every afternoon, and look away again, busy with the demands of getting by.

I dip my brush and grimly slop on the Armour-All, over the big smiles and laughing eyes and joined hands, sealing them all in behind a clear surface that promises to dry diamond-hard.

'What a great event,' says the minister, and surveying the gymnasium I can see that, yes, this is just the minister's kind of thing: authentic ethnic food on the trestle tables, a welcoming song by the East Timorese choir, real grassroots community development in the shape of a hundred and thirty or so attendees. In an estate of eighteen hundred, that's hardly a throng, but the minister's delighted. And behind it all, towering across the long wall, the mural. Glistening bright. Just as the Queen is someone for whom the world smells like fresh paint, the minister is someone for whom the world must smell like fresh anti-graffiti sealant.

'Such a positive message,' the minister is saying, 'and I understand the community itself had a hand in creating it. Marvellous.'

A group of adolescents goes up to inspect the mural, pointing something out. These guys wanted pool tables with the grant money, and who can blame them? The two artists step up to engage them in some kind of conversation, Mandy passing a self-conscious hand through her outlandish hair as the boys look to the floor, sullen and cowed, and I think there must still be residual acetylene fumes in the air, because I'm feeling a faint itching behind the eyes, a crawling tight constriction in my throat.

'You've certainly acquitted your grant,' the minister says, as I fiddle with my drink and see the Vietnamese women in my peripheral vision serving the spring rolls, wondering if they see their faces in the mural, or something approximating them. Then I drag my eyes away from the minister's charcoal lapel to catch the wondrous sight of my fabric-painting class, filing into the room nervously and stopping the show in a blaze of embroidered hijabs and fringed shawls and gathered layered skirts, seeing me there and smiling the faint encouraging smiles of the truly dutiful, the truly kind. Yes, it's a grant acquittal to be proud of, a culturally diverse photographic wet dream, and I'm blaming the Armour-All, with its patented anti-stick, for the pricking sting now in the corners of my eyes, for the way everyone here, all of these estate residents, seems to have formed themselves, for once, into one homogeneous whole; one discreet and circumspect crowd carefully distancing themselves, with subtle and infinite dignity, from the huge sprawling image that blares at them from the wall, bright and simplistic as a colouring book.

'Thank you,' I say to the minister. 'I wonder if you'll excuse me.'

I'm on my way over to the women when the centre manager grabs my arm, flushed and expansive.

'Great!' he says, handing me the camera. He's

beckoning to the minister, grinning, glancing up at the mural to find a good place to stand in front of. 'I noticed those empty solvent tins out by the bins,' he murmurs in passing. 'Can you dispose of them somewhere else, where the kids from round here won't find them and sniff them? Ta.'

Another thought strikes him. 'And can you get some of the ladies in your Turkish group to come over here for a photo too? In front of the mural?'

Local colour is what he wants. A multicultural coup. Boxes ticked. Oh, here's our vision alright, I think bitterly, sealed and impervious and safeguarded. And no matter what gets scrawled there, whatever message or denial or contradiction, you can just wipe it away. With white spirit.

I weave through the crowd, away from him. Over to Nahir and Mawiya and Jameela.

'Here,' I say, handing the camera, against all office-equipment policy, to a surprised Jameela. 'I have to go soon, so you take this.'

Her eyes widen. 'To take ... what?'

'Whatever you like. Just point and press.'

I turn to leave, heavy-footed across the gymnasium floor, drained of energy. To collect those empty cans from the skip and then drive home, head out the window, car full of dizzying, flammable solvent vapours. To sling them into my own bin, in my own less-desperate suburb.

I'm at the door before I hear Jameela calling my name. She's hurrying up behind me, reaching to take my arm firmly, steering me determinedly back into the waiting group of the painting class, who have assembled themselves excitedly in a quiet corner. I stand there in the middle in my jeans and black top, a dowdy, sad sparrow among peacocks. Then as Jameela raises the camera I feel two arms on either side of me, stretching tentatively round my waist, drawing me tighter, and in spite of everything, I smile.

Little Plastic Shipwreck

Roley went down to say hi to Samson at the start of the shift, so he was the first to realise he'd died during the night. Samson was nearly twenty-five, which is pretty old for a dolphin, and as soon as Roley put down his hose and bucket next to the pool and saw the grey familiar shape floating on the surface, he had a bad feeling. He leaned his mop against the slightly peeling paint of the Oceanworld mural and crouched there at the lip of the pool, gazing at Samson, faithful old crowd-pleaser. Hoping he died in his sleep, if dolphins even slept. Nobody was really sure, or so his boss Declan declared during his dolphin-show spiel at eleven o'clock each day.

'A popular theory,' he'd say in that golly-gee voice he put on, 'is that only one side of their brains sleeps at a time! The other side stays awake and keeps them breathing!'

There used to be Samson and another dolphin, Jiff, in the show, but that was long before Roley's time. If the Oceanworld mural was to be believed, once upon a time there'd actually been four fit and shining dolphins leaping into the air above the aqua sparkle of the dive pool, two girls in bikinis holding rings outstretched. Roley didn't think they'd bother to paint over the image now that Samson was gone. After all, it showed the stand jam-packed with summer tourists too, which was wishful thinking in anyone's books. And if Lara and Kaz, the two women who worked at Oceanworld, ever togged up in outfits like the ones in the mural, there'd be a stampede for the exits, in his opinion.

He wondered if he should start draining the pool now, on the slim chance any tourists actually walked through the gate and had their day ruined, off the bat, by a dead dolphin. After all, people sued Disneyland for less. And Oceanworld, clearly, was teetering on the edge of bankruptcy anyway; a sad cluster of concrete pools and enclosures surrounded on all sides by murals depicting a far bigger, shinier aquatic adventure park, like those billboards of sleek apartment blocks which were nailed up around the shabby prefab bunkers on building sites. It was only once you'd paid your money and clicked through the chrome turnstiles and properly looked around, scenting that whiff of rotten fish on the air, that you realised you'd been had.

When Roley's wife, Liz, had come home from the hospital she'd walked cautiously, as if she was still hooked up to machines. She'd cast a fearful look behind her, or wait in a doorway before entering a room. They hadn't taken any of her brain out, the doctors had explained to Roley; they were definite on that point. They'd put her in an induced coma until the brain swelling went down, then somehow pieced those sections of her skull back together. How did they do it? Riveting? Gluing? Roley had no idea. He imagined them with a tiny Black & Decker, a wisp of smoke rising, putting in a neat line of holes then stitching it with wire. His imagination used to run away with him, sitting there in the hospital chair beside her bed, everything toothpaste-coloured, everything smelling like Dettol. An induced coma.

Roley's brain hadn't been working too well itself, that day they sat him down in the Special Room to listen to the surgeon. That room set up an edgy little thrum in him, full of bad vibrations. The blondewood veneer table all by itself in the bare room. A single box of tissues on it. The last thing you wanted to see when you came in. He'd been trying to listen to what they were saying while all the time he was imagining some lowly admin person there at the hospital, who handled purchasing and requisitions, making sure those tissues were always in stock. So that he found himself saying, 'I'm sorry, can you just repeat that,' but unable to stop thinking of the meeting that decided a bare room provisioned with Kleenex was needed, somewhere you could close the door on and deliver the news then walk out of, busy, blameless, relieved, leaving the person inside to think about a head being wired together.

Funny what did you in, Roley thought. Not the shaved head and blanket stitch holding the edges of that tender scalp together, not Liz's black eyes and the spreading bruise on her forehead, mulberry dark, radiating from the spot where the skin had split open like someone dropping a melon on concrete (*Stop thinking like that*, Roley had ordered himself savagely, *just stop it now*, forcing himself to look calmly into her eyes and not hear that wet thwack of impact), no, it was the hair that remained that killed him, poking through bandages, still with the dye on the ends, the blonde streaks she'd paid seventy bucks for back in a time when she looked in a mirror and still cared enough.

Six weeks before.

Once she got home she had a hard time even finding the word for mirror. Sometimes he'd catch her sitting looking out the window, half a cup of tea undrunk on the table in front of her, running her hand slowly over her face as if memorising its shape. Either marvelling, Roley thought, that it was all in one piece, or else unsure that she was all there, after being helpless in the hands of strangers who could put her in or out of a coma at will.

Declan swore long and low when he came over and looked into the pool.

'Use the chains,' he said dismissively. 'I reckon that thing weighs one hundred and fifty kilos. Haul it out and then drain the pool.'

'What will I do with him?' Roley couldn't help the personal pronoun, wasn't going to call Samson an 'it'.

Declan, during his show spiel, always went on and on about the special bond between humans and dolphins, how he'd trained the dolphins here at Oceanworld, how they could divine his moods. Speaking in the plural as if nobody in the scattered audience noticed there was just Samson, cruising along the bottom waiting for the precise moment when Roley would drop his hand into the bucket for the fish that would bring him slaloming through the water to start his routine. Roley would crouch at the edge of the platform, following Declan's repertoire of gestures and punchlines, the rhetorical questions ('And do you know WHY they breathe that way, kids? I'll tell you why!') until he reached the point in the script where he'd say, 'Well, now, a dolphin can stay underwater for up to FIFTEEN MINUTES, but luckily for us here today Samson can't wait to meet you!' and Roley would reach casually into the bucket and Samson would arc up like clockwork and break the surface, his calm, loving eye on Roley alone.

Roley had a theory that the reason visitors loved Samson so much was that he was the only creature at the aquarium who seemed to be able to create a facial expression, apart from the sea-lion Rex, whose eyes were so fogged over with milky-blue cataracts ('Here, ladies and gentlemen, is old Rex — he's retired here at Oceanworld because as you can see he's lost his EYESIGHT, which means he would never survive in the wild') like something out of *Village of the Damned*, with breath that would knock you out. Poor Rex. He'd skim up on the slippery concrete and plop back into the water to turn himself around and do it again, back and forth compulsively, like a big fat kid alone on the slide. Calculating the far wall of his pool by memory. 'What's he doing?' kids would ask as they watched him, and their parents would look grimly for a few moments and then answer, 'Playing.'

The turtles were totally vacant — they had the hateful, icy glare of an old drunk — and of course the fish had no expression whatsoever. Just looked at you as they cruised past, a vegetable with fins. No short-term memory, that's what Kaz said when he told her his theory.

'That's the cliché, right?' she said, tapping the glass of one of the tanks. 'Nothing going on. You put one in a fishbowl, and they start swimming around in circles, and every time it's like: *Look, a little plastic shipwreck!* Five seconds later: *Look, a little plastic shipwreck!*'

And the penguins, even the ones with the little tufty eyebrows, still had to quirk their whole heads even to convey a response. Mostly they just looked shifty. Gimlet-eyed, thought Roley, whatever that meant. Whatever gimlets were. Something ice-cold, anyway, that twisted in deep.

'Get the chains,' Declan said again, staring down at Samson and down the barrel of an even crappier Oceanworld.

'Don't you have to notify the wildlife authority,' said Roley, 'and fill out paperwork or something?'

'Yeah, thanks, I think I know how to manage my own regulations. Just get it into the freezer room so nobody sees it when we open the gates.'

'I'll bury him,' said Roley, and Declan gave him a penguin look.

'Nah, cut it up,' he said, 'once it's frozen.'

And Roley nodded, keeping his face studiously neutral, thinking, *No way in the world, buddy.*

He got Kaz to help him roll Samson's body onto a wheeled pallet to get him into the coolroom, the two of them staggering at the massive blubbery dead weight of him ('An average bottlenose dolphin in these waters can weigh up to one hundred and ninety kilograms!'), with Kaz running for towels to cover the body, giving him a tearful smile.

'Remember that day in the school holidays? God, Roley, me and Lara were trying so hard not to laugh.'

Roley grinned, remembering the dolphin show, Declan hammering on about echolocation.

'That's how dolphins explore their watery world — locating objects by their ECHOES!' he'd declaimed. 'Sound travels four-and-a-half times faster in water than it does in air, and the dolphin can send out a series of clicks that bounce back to it in SOUNDWAVES to find their prey!' He wiggled his hand through the air. 'Now, kids! In a minute you will see on Samson's head a kind of big FOREHEAD called a melon! That's right! And Samson uses this melon like a special sort of LENS, to project the sound in a BEAM like a laser, which transmits clicks and receives ECHOES. And that's why we call it ECHOLOCATION!'

Roley had watched Samson, slipping along under the water, waiting.

'Is a dolphin a FISH?' Declan demanded relentlessly to a few listless headshakes in the audience. 'NO, it's a MAMMAL, like you and me! A dolphin can stay underwater for up to fifteen minutes, but luckily for us here today Samson can't wait to meet you! Who's ready to say hello to him?'

Like a game-show host, he'd flung out a hand towards the pool, but Roley — he couldn't have said why, didn't have an answer when he was carpeted about it later — didn't reach for the fish on cue. Samson's dark shape continued its underwater circuit and the ragged applause petered out.

'Well, Samson must be feeling a bit mischievous today!' Declan said with a tight smile. 'Sometimes he doesn't like obeying commands, and that does prove to us that dolphins are HIGHLY INTELLIGENT with a WILL OF THEIR OWN ...'

Roley's hand moved, and Samson exploded out of the water, curved suspended and effortless above the surface, before coming down with a mighty bellywhacker, which showered the first three rows of spectators. As Roley's hand closed around a cold fish he heard real laughter and applause as Samson's shining head appeared and he opened his ever-grinning mouth for it.

Roley had almost got the sack that day, the one day of work at the aquarium he'd actually enjoyed. But he'd apologised and submitted to being given a second chance. Where else was he going to find a part-time job that let him get home at three o'clock in the afternoon?

'Can you stop doing night shifts?' Liz's rehab therapist had asked him in the second month. 'She says it makes her really nervous, waking up when you're not there.' This, when Roley still had the well-paying job at the munitions plant, managing the midnight shift. He thought about the induced coma, how it would feel waking up remembering that's where you'd been, and put in his notice.

These days he gently woke her and got her sorted before driving down to Oceanworld to break shards of packed dead fish out of the freezer and get them into buckets, and wipe away the wriggling lines the catfish made as they sucked their way through algae on the insides of the big glass tanks.

Sometimes at night he'd feel Liz's hand land uncertainly on him and graze back and forth. Like seagrass on a current, it felt to him, and just as random. He'd take her hand and imagine silvery bubbles escaping from their mouths, floating up towards the ceiling fan, him keeping his breaths measured and even.

A party, that's where the accident had happened. Friends celebrating the installing of a jacuzzi. Except that the day was colder than expected, and people weren't getting into the jacuzzi, and so had wandered, in that way groups of people unthinkingly do, out to the decking on the other side of the house, presently unfinished. They'd stepped through the sliding doors barred pointlessly with two chairs because the thing had no railing, and his lovely, witty wife, looking for a way to help out, had taken a heavy platter out there to pass around and, turning round to answer someone's stupid question, had stepped straight off the edge of the deck, falling to the ground below. Only a metre and a half, but her head struck a rock, one of three artfully arranged boulders placed there for landscaping. He recalled the strange frozen look his friends who owned the house had when the ambulance arrived, as if they were rehearsing stories they would be telling their lawyers very soon. 'Nobody's fault,' Roley kept saying, breathing fast through his mouth, panting, he couldn't help it. 'It's barely a metre and a half,' his host kept repeating, a friend of eighteen years, while his wife picked assorted marinated olives off the grass, and the ambos immobilised Liz in a hard plastic body brace, buckling it tight, folding her arms across her chest like it was a sarcophagus, as Roley gasped oxygen, and every time he circled the stunned minute of what had happened, it hit him afresh, obliterating everything else so he had to learn it again, piece by piece.

Roley was thinking about this — he couldn't help thinking about it — as he opened the coolroom doors and made his way to the pallet inside. He crouched down to rest his hand on Samson's round, perfectly evolved head, and stroked his fingers across the blowhole that, if Samson were alive, would be too sensitive to touch.

With a jerk the doors were hauled open and Declan stood there. 'I told you to freeze it and cut it up,' he said, as Roley looked at Samson's grey flank, noticing the nicks and cuts on it, the marks and old scars. He thought, sick with grief, about the way his wife's fingers sought out the small secret place under her hair where there was a tiny dent, still. He laid his hand on that flank, feeling its muscle, and he heard the moment waiting, and said into it, 'You fucking do it.'

There was a short, boiling silence.

'I'm going to pay you till the end of the week,' spat Declan, 'and then you're out of here.'

'No problem. I'm going now,' and he stood up and shouldered his way back out into the sunshine. He'd write a card to Kaz, he thought, as he collected his jacket and headed through the kiosk and souvenir shop, a few tourists watching him blankly as he scooped up a bunch of made-in-China key rings and pens on his way through.

'What do you think you're doing?' called Declan, who'd followed him in, and Roley called cheerfully, 'Severance pay,' smiling at Declan's wife standing mouth-open at the register as he added more worthless junk to the brimming fistful he'd shoved into his pockets and clutched in the crook of his arm — a t-shirt, a stuffed toy seal, a dolphin bath toy, a couple of snowdomes filled with penguins and igloos. Seeing Samson's merry eye ('Dolphins are intelligent and playful!'), busting with some private joy as he slid himself onto the platform and expelled a hard breath through his blowhole, that eye holding Roley's own before moving to his hand in the bucket, full of such understanding, and such forgiveness.

Liz turned her head from the window as he entered.

'I'm home early,' he said.

'Are you?' she replied.

'Can I get you anything?' he said, emptying his pockets onto the dining-room table, watching her stop and consider, slow as a tide turning.

'No,' she said finally, 'there's nothing I want,' and Roley thought, that's right, there's nothing: want was what they had taken out of her, back when they were assuring him nothing was removed.

She looked at him, the scar across her forehead giving her a permanently quizzical expression, as if she was raising her eyebrows knowingly, ironically; a look long gone.

'Here,' he said cheerfully, 'I got you this.' He gave her one of the snowdomes, and as she held it he realised she was the first person he'd ever seen cradling one and not shaking it. She just held it obediently with that emptied, passive face, gazing at the plastic penguins inside.

What they should put in them, thought Roley, is a little brain, something to knock around uselessly in that bubble of fluid as snow swirled down ceaselessly and never stopped, while some big hand somewhere just kept on shaking.

Waiting

The horoscope page lying limp in my hands tells me everything will align for me at a time I least expect it, so I flip it over to the page that's about cakes and slices ideal for school lunches, then back again, riffling through a whole chunk of pages, to the blurry photos of some celebrity's thigh. She splashes in a shallow ocean and the world, apparently, speculates on whether or not that shadow there is cellulite. You can see how much they've blown up the photo, how far away they must have been, snapping the light and shade on her leg, the distant shifting shadows as she steps into the waves. There's another magazine beside me on the table in the pile, a month or two after this one, where the same celebrity's on the cover, still in a bikini, looking momentarily nonplussed. *Give us some privacy,* says the caption, and I think, *Lady, if you want privacy, stop cashing the cheques. Stop posing there with your manicured hand on your skinny hip. If you sincerely want the world to leave you alone until it forgets all about you, come and live at my place.*

They're not going to call my number for a while, which is why I'm leafing through these magazines. Here's the only place I ever read them. These ones are all over a year old, which isn't surprising in a public hospital department. What is surprising is that people have taken the time to painstakingly fill out the Find-a-Words and grade-four-level Celebrity Crosswords, people sitting right here, maybe with a lot preying on their minds, their eyes searching over a grid of letters, forwards, backwards, diagonally, hunting those letters, waiting for a sequence to jump out at them and make sense and turn into a recognisable word. They feel grimy, these magazines. Read and re-read and nervously read again with sweaty hands.

They'll call my name and I'll know then if I've got the woman instead of one of the men — there's four of them working here — and if I have I will feel ridiculous gratitude as I walk in there, that small mercy. Here's what the men do: they put the gel on and apologise that it's cold and then run the transducer over, looking only at the screen, which they don't turn around to you, because they've glanced at your ultrasound request form and they've read the doctor's code and they know what you're here to find out. No matter how hard you look at them, they hardly ever meet your eye, just move that mouse back and forth, clicking now and then with it. And if you break and say, *Please, is it still alive*, they say what they've been trained to say, so you can't blame them, but still. They clear their throat and reply, *Your doctor will discuss these results with you.* This while they're looking inside you, that's the ironic part. This careful professional detachment while they're gazing at the human map of you, the intimate, failed, faltering misstep, in ghostly black and white. White cloud coursing grainily over a black landmass, some cyclone gathering its bleary force offshore.

But one time I had the woman, and I didn't even have to ask her. She moved the transducer and gazed at the screen and then her hand came out and squeezed my leg and she looked at me and said, *I'm so sorry, I can't see a heartbeat.*

Her hand there for comfort. Warmth and pulse flowing between us, skin to skin.

She let me lie there for a little while too, and pull myself together. Maybe that's why she doesn't seem to be here anymore, maybe she let each appointment run too long. Maybe with more and more patients waiting outside, her efficient male colleagues started to get resentful that they were working through the queues so much faster than she was.

Anyway, it's been men the last three times. I'm a veteran at this now.

Lie there and have your fears confirmed, verbally or with that courteous, revealing brush-off. Get yourself back out into the waiting room to wait for the report to be printed, go up to the counter, pay for it all. After you get your Medicare refund up the street, the whole thing costs you seventy-five dollars. They don't bother giving you the actual ultrasound films now. Well, they don't bother giving them to me, anyhow. *Nothing to see*, one of them told me once, dismissively. *It's so tiny in these early stages.* Once, though, the girl at the counter handed me a disc along with my receipt. She hadn't read the report, obviously, just saw the *Gynaecological Ultrasound* printed there and burned it off for me. Thinking I'd be going home to excitedly push it into a DVD player and watch my baby jumping on the screen, healthy, identifiable. Viable.

I'll have to tell them, today, I don't want a DVD. I know what's coming. I reached ten weeks last Tuesday, day seventy, and I was standing in the kitchen chewing on a piece of toast, Pete long up and gone, feeding out the last of the hay to the cattle in the top block. I stood there rubbing at a spot on the bench wondering why the dread under the surface was pushing at me more insistently, just scratching at the cork of my bottled-up terror, and it dawned on me.

No nausea. Dull anguish like a bitter taste in my mouth, heart like a shallow dish of water I was desperate not to tip, filling my chest. That estuarine feeling of something ebbing away; those symptoms that had kept me so stupidly hopeful. Evaporating like a rainless cloud. Giving up the ghost. The spot I was rubbing slid from the bench to the back of my hand and I realised it was light, a spot of light reflected off a bottle on the windowsill. Everything was so quiet.

They won't find a heartbeat.

My doctor just fills out a request form for me now. I don't have to make an appointment to get it, so I told Pete I was coming up here to do some shopping. Pete's got enough on his plate. It's funny, in the pamphlets they hand you they talk about giving yourself permission to grieve and taking time for yourself, but they never talk much about your partner. I'm not pretending I know what it's like for him, but I look at his face and I can see that he's worn down as it is, almost to the point of slippage, like a stripped screw. Turned and turned again, straining to hold things together. He put in a crop of wheat this year, gambling on a spring break which hasn't come, and I know he's thinking of doing what all the farmers around here are slowly resigning themselves to, which is giving up on the idea and letting the cattle in to eat it down. I've watched him out there some mornings, stooping down, looking at the stalks, wondering where the point of non-recovery is, where it comes and what you do once you've decided. So this time I spared him. Kept the news of those two blue lines on the test to myself. I look at the calendar and think of him out there on the tractor sowing that wheat, ten weeks ago to the day.

Understand, I'm not a martyr. When we got married my mother gave me my grandmother's wedding ring, and I looked at the back of it worn thin from years of distracted rubbing with her thumb as she waited for my grandfather to come home, every shift out of the mines. Those years of wearing away. I do the same with it now, myself. Then, last March, when we got all the way to fourteen weeks and Pete's face had lost a little of its tightness, I was loading the washing machine and felt that tide ebbing again, the way a sharp wall of sand will collapse into the flow, and I was no more able to stop it happening than I was to turn a real tide. The soak of blood, that wall caving, impossible to ever rebuild.

In the hospital afterwards Pete stood by my bed, hesitating, as they announced visiting hours were over, and I thought he was gathering his thoughts to say something, and I closed my eyes. Instead I heard him taking off his boots and jeans and shirt, leaving them in a neat pile on the chair. He lifted the stiff white sheet and just climbed in beside me. My husband is an undemonstrative man and that gesture, as he fitted his warm arms and legs around me in the narrow bed, made me see how much he understood. I woke up in the night and felt his thumb, as he slept, absently rubbing the skin on my own arm. Oh, it wears us thin, marriage. It knocks the edges off us.

But I'm not a martyr, just someone who can see what needs doing, and does it. I've learned this from him.

The magazine's telling me there are ten steps to a new me. I turn to the page showing a rail-thin actress with a chalky-white arrow directed at her abdomen. *Baby bump?* asks the caption. I go back to the horoscopes. After I get out of here I will get the Medicare refund and put it back in the bank and then spend some time in the op-shop searching for something I could conceivably claim cost me seventy-five dollars. *Do you want a D&C*, my doctor will say, putting down the ultrasound results with a sigh, *or do you want to wait and let things take their natural course?* It's harder to explain away a day procedure in hospital so I'll take the natural course.

The natural course. Nature's way. I'm baffled by it, I don't mind telling you. I've had a gutful of it. Carving its erosion gullies through us, whipping the rug out from under us, making us eat its dust. I'm waiting for something comprehensible to jump out of this garbled mess and make sense to me. Here is the natural course, now — calling my name. The radiographer with my file, scanning the faces from the door. Blue shirt, polite smile, male. Here it comes. I rise and walk towards the examination suite for what I know is waiting for me in there. I count my steps. *Ten steps to a new me. Ten days to a flatter stomach.*

I know what Pete will be doing at home right now. He's making the decision to open the gate into the pasture with its desiccated, knee-high wheat. Can't stand its hopeful greenness struggling in that parched ground, knowing what three more days of this heat are going to do.

Let it go. Let the cows eat it.

He stands there postponing the moment when he lifts the catch on that gate, scrutinising the sky and the horizon one last time as the cattle cluster on the other side looking hungry and, oh, Pete, I know what you need and I can't give it to you; I can see it in the way you scratch the dog's tilting head just where he loves it, the thwarted tenderness of that gesture so familiar to me that I feel the heavy dish of water in my chest teeter and almost overbalance, and I ache with holding it steady.

I see it in the resigned way you take off your hat to wipe the dirt and sweat from your forehead and, with decisive and methodical force of habit, seeing what needs to be done, how you set it back straighter on your head, ready.

Static

'Anthony,' says his mother, 'what's this we're drinking?'

He'd known this was going to happen, the minute Marie showed him the punch recipe.

'You know they're hyper-conservative,' he'd said. She'd rolled her eyes, put a post-it note reminder on the recipe page and added it to her list.

'For crying out loud, what's not to like about melon ginger punch?' she'd muttered. The glossy magazine bristled with post-it notes, annotated painstakingly by Marie with dozens of clever and simple Christmas lunch suggestions for people with more to do than slave over a hot stove, et cetera.

Now his mother prods a perfectly spherical melon ball in her drink, and looks at him as if it was a floating dead mouse.

'It's punch,' Anthony says, smiling hard.

'Just something cool and refreshing,' adds Marie.

Anthony's father Frank puts his down and pulls himself off the lounge chair. 'How about a beer, son?'

'Sure, if that's what you're after.'

Anthony listens to the asthmatic wheeze of the leather chair his father's just vacated, sucking back air into itself as if desperate for breath, the only noise in the room for a few seconds. In the deoxygenated silence, he feels what he thinks of as Evil Rays, like something in one of his old comics, jagged lightning bolts shooting across the room. They're crackling from the fingertips of the archenemies seated on either side of him. *Take that, Ice Maiden! No, you take THAT, Bitch Crone!*

Then both of them, his mother and Marie, turning the Evil Rays onto him, as if the entire thing is his idea, his fault, when all he's done is get out his credit card to pay for the whole bloody shebang: the punch and the Peruvian glass punchbowl it's in and the gourmet chestnut stuffing mix in the organic free-range turkey out there, rolled and boned for easy slicing — Anthony knows exactly how it feels — and the sighing, put-upon lounge suite still on the *interest-free nothing more to pay for ten months* plan, which Marie is already obsessing is the wrong shade of taupe. Are there actually different shades of taupe? It's news to him. Hell would be like that, he thinks, gulping punch. It would be shades of taupe that drove you screaming into eternal torment, not the flames.

'Let's open the presents,' he suggests.

'But the children haven't even arrived,' says his mother.

'I meant just ours,' he answers feebly. True, for a few seconds there, he had forgotten the children were coming. His sister's offspring would dominate the day, though it wasn't the kids' fault — they'd be desperate to escape into the study as soon as they could to play with the Wii he'd bought them, the poor little buggers. No, they would be used, the children, as deflector shields against the Evil Rays, as ammunition against the day's parries and thrusts of emotional blackmail. Hannah and Tom. They'd have to be twelve and ten now.

Marie hadn't even wanted them to come; she made a big fuss about having to plan a special menu for them and how they'd turn the house upside down, but Anthony, ducking his chin and ploughing through a veritable snowstorm of Evil Rays, insisted that if they were going to have a family Christmas, his sister and her husband and kids had to be there, or his parents wouldn't show up.

'I don't care if we have KFC,' he'd finally said, gesturing to the pile of magazines hawking sunshine and patios and people in uncrushed white linen shirts. 'If we've agreed to do it, they have to come.' And Marie had slammed off into the study to channel her fury into pumping six kilometres out of the exercise bike. You could bounce a coin off her calf muscles, if you were game to try.

Rays, rays. One drills into the back of his skull as he leaves the kitchen, another counterattacks with a zap square in the solar plexus as he carries in a platter of smoked-salmon blinis. Marie's doused them with chopped dill, and his mother looks at them like they've been sprayed with grass clippings from the mower. She can get every secret weapon into those rays — contempt, accusation, disdain, puzzled faux-innocence, the works. Anthony is determined, fully determined, to thwart her with unrelenting good cheer today.

'Pikelets, eh?' says his father, eyes swivelling back to the one-day match, luridly coloured on the plasma screen. 'Well, well.' He folds one into his mouth to keep the peace while his mother refuses, mouth like a safety pin. Vol-au-vents, that's his mother's style. Cheese straws and a sherry.

Anthony starts eating the things so that when Marie comes back it will look like they've been a success. He's got four in his mouth when a stray caper lodges itself in his throat and forces him to cough a spray of ricotta and dill and masticated pancake into a Christmas napkin. For a second he's terrified he might actually throw up, and wouldn't that be a wonderful start to the day, but he swallows down a mouthful of punch and his stomach settles.

Where's Marie? If there's one thing those magazines kept promising, it was that even though you were a hostess you wouldn't need to be tied to the kitchen all morning; with your new fresh and fun easy-peasy celebration menu you'd be relaxing with those you loved on this special day.

He can't go back out to the kitchen yet. It wouldn't look right. 'Who's winning, Dad?' he says.

'The Pakis.'

On the screen the tiny bright figures move as if they're underwater. Bowl and deflect. Go back, wait, run up slowly, bowl and … block. Christ, it's like watching paint dry.

'I got all my shopping done early and out of the way this year,' says his mother. 'And what a relief that was. I can't stand having to shop when the place is such a madhouse just before Christmas.'

'You're right. It's crazy, isn't it?' He recalls going to Safeway just the night before, running up and down the aisles searching for cranberries in syrup. The person ahead of him at the check-outs was buying four barbeque chickens, salad mix and a big tub of choc-chip ice-cream, and Anthony had felt an overwhelming, childish longing to follow them out and curl up in the back of their car and go home to their place.

'And I got everything boxed,' his mother is saying, 'just big square boxes. I'll never forget the terrible problems we had wrapping that rocking horse for Tom.' Seven years later, and she's still talking about it.

'What did you get him this year?' says Anthony. He can see the packages under the tree — all the same red paper with identical bows.

'A walkie-talkie set.' She looks at him shrewdly, and Anthony does his best to simulate admiring delight.

'Oh! He'll … Was that something he said he wanted?'

'You know how much he loves all his electronic games.

He'll be able to play police games with this, with his friends. You know, hiding round the house.'

'Terrific.'

She's on to him in an instant. 'What? Don't you think it's a good idea? Lord knows it cost me enough. I just try to keep up with what the children seem to want; I don't know all the latest gadgets. I just do my best.'

God, where is Marie? 'No, no. It's a great idea. He'll love it.'

When Tom sees the Wii, Anthony knows, the walkie-talkie's going to get dropped like a dud Tamagotchi.

'I'll just see if Marie needs a hand,' he says, weaving through the lounge chairs to the kitchen.

'Honestly,' he hears his mother tut as he exits, 'how hard is it to roast a turkey?'

Listless applause sounds from the TV as someone finally hits something, and the lounge chair exhales a gust of weary depression.

Marie's face, as she glances up, is murderous.

'Pit those,' she snaps, flicking her eyes to some cherries. 'If your father cracks a filling on a cherry pip I'll never hear the end of it.'

She's — what the hell's she doing? Anthony stares at his wife's hand, vanished to the wrist inside a Christmas ham.

'I'm getting the fat and skin off. I'm not going to drop dead of cholesterol even if they all want to.' She extracts her hand like a doctor completing an internal exam and peels back the great flapping layer of fat. 'Look at that. Disgusting.' She wraps it in a plastic bag, shuddering, and drops it into the bin. 'We'll just have this ham cold, sliced and arranged on the platter with some rocket garnish and a scattering of cranberries.'

Anthony grimaces. He can hear the pitch rising in her voice, the manic brittleness that has nowhere to go but up, up, up into hectic hysteria. It will break later, after everyone has gone, and the tic that's jumping now under her eye will somehow afflict her whole face and pump itself down her arms and legs.

'Try not to get upset,' he says as calmly as he can. 'I'll do all that before we eat, just come in and sit down for a while.'

She's scrubbing ham grease off her hands in the sink. 'I hate that lounge suite,' she mutters. 'I told you it was the wrong colour.'

Anthony scrabbles in the cutlery drawer for the cherry pitter he remembers buying at Ikea. 'So I'll just do these cherries then.'

'I'm not going back in there by myself,' says Marie, who fronts a whole courtroom five days a week.

'Well,' says Anthony, keeping it light with everything he has, 'I'll bring this bowl in, and do them in there.'

'Are you serious?'

'Sure. It'll give my mother something to correct me about. Make her happy.'

She flashes him a smile as she heads for the door. The ghost of an old smile, one he misses; she's trained herself not to do it because it shows the tooth she's convinced is crooked. He's told her he loves that tooth, but she just rolls her eyes. In every one of their wedding photos, stored over there in the hand-tooled leather albums, she has on the other smile, the trained one — lips closed and chin raised like a model of cool serenity, a perfected study of herself. But somewhere in a drawer, Anthony has an old photo of her, pulling off her mask and snorkel at the Great Barrier Reef, just out of the water and her grin broad and unselfconscious. Years ago.

'I don't have any explanation for it,' she'd told the fertility specialist last week when they had their first session. 'I'm doing everything right: diet, exercise, monitoring ovulation …'

How reasonable she'd sounded, how level-headed. That lawyer's tilt to her head, the voice pleasant and determinedly non-aggrieved. And the specialist nodded and said, 'Sometimes these things take more time than we expect,' and she'd replied, in a voice a shade or two firmer, that she'd done her own research and was ready for the first stage of conception enhancement.

That was the term she'd used: *conception enhancement*. Like they were joining the Scientologists rather than trying to make a baby.

Anthony takes the cherry bowl and the Ikea pitter and an extra saucer into the lounge room and sits at the end of the dining-room table. Marie is at the stereo, riffling through the stack of CDs for something suitable, his mother pointedly brushing dill off a blini she holds in her palm.

'Aren't you the domestic one?' says his mother when she sees him, and he waits, counting tiredly to himself, and getting to seven before she adds, 'Just watch you don't splatter that shirt with cherry juice because it's the devil's own to get out.'

He starts on the first cherry, and his mother writhes with the discomfort of not interfering.

'Would you like me to do it?' she blurts when she can no longer endure it after ten seconds.

'No, thanks but no. I'm enjoying the challenge.'

The cherry stones drop onto the saucer, and the repetition of the task lulls Anthony into a light trance. The cherries are huge, bigger than any he remembers from his childhood. He and his sister Margaret used to sit on the back step and eat them, collecting the stones for that rhyming game about who you'd marry, and Margaret would always eat the exact number required to get her past *tinker, tailor, soldier, sailor*, all the way to *rich man*. He remembers spiking her pile with an extra stone, just to bump it up to *poor man* and drive her crazy.

It's worked too, that trick. She and Ian are in some dire financial straits. He's under oath to say nothing to their parents, but it makes him feel uncomfortable, having the big new house, and that's what made him overcompensate, probably, with the presents. Thunk, thunk, go the cherry stones, sliding obediently from the dripping flesh. Slippery as hard little rocks you'd remove from someone's gall bladder. In fact, one time he'd had his ears syringed after they'd blocked up during a bad cold, and he was astonished to hear a thunk into the kidney dish the doctor had instructed him to hold beside his head. Looking down as the warm solution sloshed around inside his ear, he saw a hard ball of wax just the size and shape of one of these cherry stones lying there. Anthony couldn't believe something like that had been wedged in his ear all along, slowly building up like a small, solid boulder. And what amazed him even more was the sudden clearing of sound as the water drained from his ear canal. It was like finding the treble knob on your sound system at last and hearing, really hearing, everything that had been dulled and muted before.

'I hope you don't mind our funny little present to you, Marie,' says his mother. 'It's just that you're so hard to buy for, the two of you — I mean, my goodness, there's really absolutely nothing else you need, is there?'

'No,' says Marie, smiling that gracious close-lipped smile. 'We've both worked hard to get the house the way we want it, haven't we, Anthony?'

Tinker, tailor, soldier, sailor, he counts before he answers. 'Yep, but it's been worth it,' he says. *Rich man, poor man, beggar man, thief.* You couldn't have that rhyme now — kids wouldn't get it. You'd have to update it. *IT, banker, accountant, defence-force personnel ... human-resources manager ...*

She used to call him Ant. He can't put his finger on when it started being Anthony. It was like his attention had waned momentarily, and then there it was, a new name and a new smile, to go with the new granite-topped Italianate kitchen bench and the whole brand spanking new house. He'd closed his eyes signing the mortgage on the house, suffering a brief swooping dizzy spell of nauseated disbelief, and he thinks of that title document now stacked away in some bank vault somewhere, his signature slumping below the dotted line like a failing ECG.

The front doorbell rings its two-gong Tibetan chime, and he jumps up.

'That'll be Margaret and Ian!' he cries, making for the door just as his mother rests her hand thoughtfully on the upholstered lounge chair, readying herself for the next bout, and says, 'What colour do you call this, Marie?'

At the table Anthony stands hunched, looking through the viewfinder of his digital camera. He's starting to breathe a bit easier now, with lunch almost finished. He looks at the group of them reproduced in pixels, their movements at the table making the image shift and shimmer like a 3-D postcard.

'Oh, good, get some photos,' calls his mother, a little loud now after three white wines. 'Get one of all of us,

Anthony. 'There's so few occasions we're all together like this.' She waves her hand extravagantly to bring Tom and Hannah over beside her and gestures again at Anthony. 'Put it on the timer thing and be in the photo too; get a record of all of us before we all change forever.' She's gone a bit slurred and maudlin, he sees with alarm — blinking hard and giving her eyes a surreptitious blot on one of Marie's linen napkins. 'Time goes so fast,' she says to nobody in particular.

Anthony stands tilting the camera a few millimetres back and forth, mesmerised, as the group arranges itself before him. The pixellated image oscillates, scanning and reading the shifts of light and shade. One moment he sees his sister, overweight and worn and dowdy in her Target outfit, frumpy beside the immaculate blonde Marie, who outshines them all. The next he sees Margaret, kind and comfortable, touching Ian's arm and smiling warmly, with Marie pale and cold and stick-thin, face grimaced into a close-mouthed rictus. Back and forth the shimmering image goes; how she sees them and how they see her, this life and that life, with Anthony in the middle, trying to hold the camera steady and depress the button for auto-focus at the same moment. He's looking at the faces of his niece and nephew as he takes the picture, the way they're holding their smiles frozen, crouched compliant beside his mother, waiting for it to be over. Where do we learn those smiles from, Anthony is thinking as he preserves it all, megabyte by megabyte.

'Now, Tom,' he says to his nephew as they're clearing away after lunch. 'I really hope you enjoy your presents and everything, but I just need to have a quiet word with you, man to man.'

'OK,' Tom says. He's trying hard to behave himself today, dressed up in new shirt and jeans. Brand-new, like he got them that morning, and it makes Anthony's heart contract in small, constricting aches to think the kids have got good clothes this year for their Christmas presents.

'I've bought you a present I reckon you'll love, and I think you'll really want to play with it, but the thing is, Grandma's also got you a present she'd like you to play with, and I think it would be nice if just for today you played with hers. OK?'

'Why?'

Why indeed? Why is he pandering to the domineering old harridan? She's just spent Christmas lunch behaving as if it's a cardinal sin not to serve roast parsnips. Asking for a cup of tea, of all things, instead of dessert, sending Marie back out to the kitchen to make it specially. Why is he trying to embroil Tom in this too?

'Well, she's tried hard to get you something she thinks you'll like, you see. The thing I've got you'— he gives Tom a big indulgent-uncle grin — 'let's say you need a TV for it, but we can play it anytime, my place or your place.'

'I don't think we have the right attachment thing for it,' says his nephew, his face beginning to fall. 'Our TV's too old. If it's a Wii, I mean.'

'Right,' says Anthony, owner of three plasma wide-screens, possessor of a seven-figure debt, master juggler of every line of credit. He's smiling hard again now, his face feeling numbed with it. 'Right, well. I'll have a talk to your mum about maybe … um …'

How to broach it with Margaret, how to offer? Tell her he never uses the one in the bedroom? Yeah, tell her it's been sitting in the guest bedroom gathering dust, be great if she could take it off his hands. A loan. As long as they'd like it. His fault for buying the gadget. Anthony has to squeeze his hands together between his knees to stop himself grabbing Tom and hugging him as hard as he can. A thin boy. Too troubled for a ten-year-old. Reading out those stupid knock-knock jokes at the table, trying his best to do just what's expected of him, to decipher all those signals and stand in the firing line of all those deadly rays.

Later, when they're assembled in the lounge opening the presents, he winks lightning fast at Tom as he eases the sticky tape away from the walkie-talkie box.

'Thanks, Grandma!' the boy says, getting up to give her a dutiful kiss, and Anthony's praying for her to just shut up for a minute, just one fucking minute for once in her life, but she can't, of course, she has to start in on how he's got to look after it because it cost a lot of money and he can't take it to school, it's just to be played with at his house, and she accepts Tom's muted kiss on the cheek without even looking at him, not really, because what she wants are babies, she only likes them when they're babies, by the time they're Tom's and Hannah's age they've learned to be wary and submissive and not to trust her, and who can blame them?

Anthony squeezes his hands between his knees again and looks over at Marie clasping her gift basket of toiletries. He thinks of the kilometres she tries to cover each night on that stationary bike, the endless net surfing she's done on sperm motility and ovarian cysts, like someone gathering evidence for a case they have to win. Does she love him? She lets him see her in the morning without make-up, does that count?

'Batteries,' he hears himself saying as Tom takes out the two handsets from their foam boxing. 'I've got just the thing over here, wait a sec,' and he's tearing a corner off the wrapping on the Wii to dig inside for the pack of AAs he's tucked in there for the remote control.

'Do you want to have a go with Tom?' Margaret asks Hannah, who screws up her nose and shakes her head with the exquisite disdain of a twelve-year-old girl.

'Me!' Anthony says, leaping up. 'Let's check out the range on these things!'

Once he leaves, he knows the conversation could go two ways: his loyal sister, God bless her, keeping the peace and staunchly championing him as being great with kids; or his mother, voice flat with disparagement, claiming that he'll never grow up, no matter what sort of high-powered job he seems to find for himself. And what would Marie say about him? Which side would she take?

'Outside!' he calls to Tom as he sprints down the hall. He's suddenly desperate for fresh air. 'Switch yours on, see the rocker switch?'

'Yeah, I'm on to it,' Tom replies, disappearing into the laundry.

Anthony hears him stop and begin to negotiate the squadron of deadlocks on the door that leads outside. He does the same with the sliding doors onto the patio and jogs down the steps to the house's north side.

They'd paid a landscaper to do the garden, and he'd dug up the grass along this whole stretch and laid down a bed of stones. Anthony's feet crunch on it now, making him stagger slightly. The stones are too big, really, to be called pebbles. It's like wading across a big, empty, bone-dry riverbed. 'Absolutely zero care,' the landscaper had said, and he'd been right. Anthony flicks on his walkie-talkie, holds it to his mouth.

'Securing the zone,' he deadpans into the mouthpiece, stifling a grin. 'Agent Two, do you copy?'

He flicks the switch and hears a snow of static, moves his arm in an arc to clear it. Rays, he thinks vaguely, are holding them together. Currents zapping between the aerials. He flicks the switch back once the static clears and tries again.

'Commando Two,' he barks. 'Do you read me?'

He hears a gurgle on the other end. His nephew, laughing. Anthony sinks to a crouch, raises the walkie-talkie to his ear, and listens. Tom's voice, when it starts through the chuckling, is so loud and tinny he almost jumps.

'Reading you, Uncle Ant,' he says, and starts laughing again.

'Commando Two, request information — who is Uncle Ant? Please repeat code name,' he rasps. He lowers his head in the shade of the pergola, his ear pressed to the handset to hear the smile again in his nephew's voice. Instead the voice he hears is Marie's, her tone hard and skating on pain like it was ice, *Well, Anthony, tonight's the night, this is the window, do you want to have a child or don't you?* and his chest tightening as he tried to think of what to answer her. Then her voice again, rising bitterly from her side of the bed, *Just say, just tell me, so I'm not wasting my time anymore*, and then Tom is giggling again, saying, 'Commando Two here, sir, reading you loud and clear,' and Anthony — gazing at the stones at his feet, then up at the glazed pots full of massed blue-grey succulents on the patio with its two canvas chairs arranged just so — finds his voice has deserted him. His throat has closed up.

Static and space wash over the line, a sound like the inside of a shell. He can see into the kitchen from here: Marie at the granite bench, straightening mince pies on a platter. She's using tongs to lift them from the cardboard box, like the woman at the ludicrously expensive bakery did, placing them reverently down in a line.

He watches his wife's face pinched with grim

concentration, remembers her voice at the end of its tether in the darkness. But tethered by what? He hears a sharp catch of breath — his own, coming through the headset. *For fuck's sake*, he tells himself, *pull yourself together*. He watches as Marie takes the sifter and starts dusting the pies with icing sugar and something dislodges in him with a delicate gush of pressure, something shifts to let bright sound in.

He watches her wrists flex, the air going out of him, certain, all of a sudden, that nothing of him will ever take root inside that thin, tightly wound body, nothing. Tom's voice comes through the handset again. Clear as a bell now, the clearest thing he's ever heard.

'Agent One?' it says, tentative. Like he thinks Anthony's given up on him already and tired of the game.

'Copy,' rasps Anthony, flipping the switch. 'Ambushed here, Commando.'

Marie turns and turns the sifter's handle, the muscle twitching in her face, resolutely dousing the pastries that nobody will want to eat with a deluge of white, a blanketing snowfall of sweetness, covering every track.

'Do you require assistance?' comes the voice at the other end of the line.

'Yes,' he says. 'Man down here. Man … inoperative.' Jesus, what's he saying? 'Over,' he adds hastily.

'I can't really hear you, Uncle Ant,' says Tom's voice. There's another bubbling of static, the distant squeaking of some other low-band frequency interfering with the line. Anthony thinks he hears Tom add, 'Can we go and play with the Wii now?'

He means to say yes. He wants just to lose himself in the big benign glowing screen, crack open Cokes for the kids and have that quiet word with Margaret and Ian, have the day mean something. He's exhausted, suddenly.

'Man down. Mayday,' he hears himself croaking instead. 'Mayday.'

OK. He's got about forty seconds before Tom comes and finds him. That's all he needs to pull this back together, summon the good energy, get up off his knees and blame the static. But he finds, in the luxury of those seconds, that he can't take his eyes off the cacti in their pots. They don't seem to have grown an inch since they were planted there at the advice of the landscaper six long months ago. Totally unchanged. Zero care.

Anthony puts the handset down onto the stones and gazes at the plants, so steely and barbed and implacable, something that even neglect and drought put together can't seem to kill. He reaches out with a fascinated finger to press a curved spike, hard, against the cushion of skin. He just wants to see a dot of hot, red blood well reliably up, as if he needs proof that such things are real.

Seventy-Two Derwents

Mrs Carlyle has given us all exercise books and said we are going to try to keep a journal this term. This is mine. She says it's better if we don't feel self-conscious so we don't have to put our names on the journals. They will be <u>anonymous</u>. She says she would just like to read them.

Mrs Carlyle has two budgies, a boy and a girl, and they have built a nest. If they have baby budgies and if I'm allowed she will give me one. You have to wait until they're old enough to leave the nest before you can take them away from their parents because they need special looking after. In my mind I can picture this. The babies would live in a soft little nest inside the milk carton Mrs Carlyle has put into their cage as a nesting box.

The nest for the budgies is soft because I think the mother bird pulls some feathers out of her chest to put inside. This seems cruel but Mrs Carlyle says she put other soft things in the cage and the mother budgie didn't want any of them. She is using <u>instinct</u>. The babies would all be snuggled up inside. If she will give one to me, I would like a girl budgie. I think I would name her Alicia. When I think about teaching her how to say her name I can nearly hear it. I have to wait, Mrs Carlyle says, because she's not sure her budgie is even going to lay eggs yet. She says not to tell the other kids because they would get jealous. After she says this, when I walk back into class and down to my desk, I feel my skin buzzing like someone has stroked it. I hope Alicia is blue.

My mum says do you like him? Shane, I mean. She has on her nice earrings. He's OK, I say. Later on when Shane comes over, Mum is in the kitchen cooking dinner. She's made homemade lasagne and now she's heating up oil in the deep saucepan. She calls to Shane you haven't lived till you've had my home-cooked chips. I'm famous for them. Isn't that right, Tyler? My home-cooked chips?

Once I asked if I could get some money to go and buy a hamburger and she suddenly jumped up really angry and said why do you need a crap takeaway hamburger? I can make you a much better hamburger here at home. She got mince out and made a hamburger in the frypan with onions. It took forever. At last she gave it to me with two pieces of bread holding it all together. Isn't that better than Maccas? she kept asking. Isn't it? Answer me.

Now I just say yes. Mrs Carlyle told us that when you are training your dog you need to say the same thing over and over until the dog gets it. He wants to do the right thing, he just doesn't know it at first. She says it's the same with training a bird to talk, you have to say the same thing again and again so they learn. That's true and maybe it's true for people too.

I'm starving, says Shane and looks over at me with a smile. He is just out of the shower and there are comb marks in his hair. He says you wanna change channels? and leans over to give me the remote. You have to press the button really hard to make it change channels now because it's wearing out. So I change it over to The Simpsons.

What grade are you in? he says, and I tell him Grade 6, Mrs Carlyle's class. 6C. She comes in and says how are you this morning, my treasures? My lovely 6Cs. I've missed you!

I don't tell Shane this. Grade 6, he repeats. When Homer and Marge talk to each other their whole heads move to ask a question and then answer but when Shane talks to me just his eyes move sideways, his head stays watching TV.

He says I bet you've got a boyfriend. I can hear my mum clattering oven trays in the kitchen. On the TV Bart is climbing up into his tree house. He can go really fast, much faster than I could in real life. Just a few steps and he's there. But I always like to see the inside of his tree house. I wish I had one. And I don't want a boyfriend. I want the set of seventy-two Derwents.

They are in a tin that opens out with all the sharp points of the pencils in order and in every colour you could ever think of using. Georgia has some at school and even when you sharpen them they feel special, the wood is so soft and it peels back to leave the pencil good as new. My grandma asked me what I wanted for my birthday and I took her to the shop where they are. The art supply shop smells so beautiful inside, all clean new pencils and paper and brushes. She had a good look at them. For your colouring in? she said. I felt happy when we walked out again, imagining. They have names soft as feathers. Pale Mint. Sea Green. Grey Green. French Grey. Rose Pink. Cloud Blue. Iced Blue. Kingfisher Blue. Prussian Blue. Indigo. Sometimes just when I am walking along the names come into my head like a rhyme in time with my footsteps.

I will put them into my denim pencil case and only take a few at a time to school, but I will invite Georgia over to my house and open up the whole tin so we can do drawing and colouring in together on the table on the weekend. Mrs Carlyle has a special Stanley knife and she could scrape some of the paint off the end so I could write my name on each one. On the tin someone's done a sketch of an old stone bridge going over a rocky creek. It is a very good drawing and it looks like a picture from the old set of encyclopaedias in the library. When I go in there

Mrs Bradbury says it's good to see someone still uses the reference section, Tyler. I think she means the lovely way the books smell, which is true, I love that too.

You have got a boyfriend, haven't you? says Shane. I can tell. Cause you're blushing.

Bart and Milhouse are in his tree house and they're talking about staying out there the night. I'm watching and I know that in a few seconds it will be night and you will see the moon and they will get scared.

In cartoons time passes really fast and sudden. Also, things happen that aren't true. Like a cat will be running along and will go through the wall and there will be an exactly cat-shaped hole left behind in the wall. Mum's old boyfriend Gary threw a bottle at the wall once and it didn't leave a shape like that it just smashed.

Bart and Milhouse are still in the tree house but it's night and there are big shadows that scare them. They race down the rope ladder screaming. When they scream on The Simpsons their mouths open way up and their little tongues come out and wriggle and you can see their tonsils. That's meant to be funny, and it must be because Shane laughs. Bart runs back into his room and hides in his bed. I like Lisa but she's not in this one.

I'm not blushing, I say to Shane. Sure looks like it to me, he says. What do you get up to with that boyfriend of yours? See, you're not looking at me, so I know it's true.

I try to think if I've ever seen a Simpsons where a

human goes running through a wall and leaves a person-shaped hole.

Wait till you taste these chips, calls my mum.

Shane is under my mum's Subaru in the driveway. What a shitheap, he says. I ask him what he's fixing up and he says the carby. He's out there for a long time even when Mum tells him to come inside and have dinner, which is just pasta tonight. It is those little shell ones. I get a clean one onto the side of my plate and imagine it is something in the sea where an animal lives. Ellie is working tonight at Subway. Shane and my mum argue outside about the car and something in the garage gets knocked over. Whatever you've taken out you'd better put back in because I need it tomorrow, says Mum, and Shane says look it's just not that simple. I could curl up inside this soft shell and it would be like a hammock in there, all warm. That's all I want to write for today.

If Georgia came over to my house we could make hot Milo and some of that popcorn that you cook in the microwave. She told me she was on camp once and they had toasted marshmallows on sticks over the fire. We could do them under the griller. We have a packet of wooden skewers. We could draw horses and do the colouring in and then we could watch Saddle Club and if she wanted we could put on some of Mum's nail polish. Even just do our homework together. I always do my homework when I come home from school. Mum says I sure didn't get that gene off her. I like to sketch but Mum says that's not going to impress the teachers and she wasn't still paying off a colour printer and a computer with internet so I could just do drawings.

First there is Home and Away then Deal or No Deal. If Georgia came over we could go into my room and Mum wouldn't keep knocking and asking me what I was doing because when you have a friend over that explains it.

And if Shane came over he would leave us alone I hope.

OK, goodbye for now.

Mrs Carlyle said who's been writing things in their diary and nobody put up their hand so I kept mine down too, just in time. Someone said there's nothing to write about and Mrs Carlyle said why not write about something that happened to you when you were little, like learning to ride a bike or Christmas or a favourite toy.

I have a doll that my Aunty Jacinta gave me for Christmas two years ago when we went to their place in the country. The doll has a long dress and hidden under the dress instead of feet is another doll and you can pull it all inside out. She is first of all like Cinderella when she was dressed in patchy clothes and when you pull the dress over the other side has Cinderella in her ball gown and she has a crown on her head. The whole doll is knitted. When my mum saw it she laughed. My older brother Zac had come with us for Christmas and she rolled her eyes at him and nudged him and said see, told you it would be like The Waltons, but Zac just said who are The Waltons? and he wouldn't look at her. I don't know Zac very well because he has lived with another family since before I was born. There's just been Ellie and me even though Mum had three other children before us, Dylan, Zac and Tegan. Anyway Zac was there and it felt strange because the cousins were all like new kids at a strange school, not talking, and my mum said I had so many dolls at home already I was just getting spoiled and to say thank you to Aunty Jacinta for the homemade one.

I said I love her, I love her crown, thank you. Aunty Jacinta leaned over and gave me a hug and she smelled so nice, not like perfume but just cups of tea and shampoo, and she said softly she doesn't have to be Cinderella, Tyler, you can give her a new name if you like. Then my mum jumped up and said are we allowed to have a glass of wine or do we have to say grace first round here.

After lunch when we got into the car to come home Zac said just drop me off at the station and Mum said I thought you were staying for a few days and he just shrugged and shook his head. Mum said there probably won't even be a train on Christmas Day and he said I checked and there is.

After we dropped him Mum said he always was an ungrateful little shit, wasn't he, Ellie? Do you remember, Ellie, how he always took his father's side? Ellie said no she couldn't remember. I wished she had just said yes because then Mum wouldn't have kept going. I knew she would and she did. All the Christmas lunch in my stomach turned into a hard cold stone as she started talking on and on about how Aunty Jacinta and Uncle Matt thought they were so great and they didn't even have a plasma and they'd always been like that, always judging her, and Jacinta had always been the favourite with Grandma and how neither of them had given her any support when she'd got pregnant with Tegan and she'd had to move out of home too young and that's what had started all the problems. Mum said they both denied it but she was sure either Jacinta or Grandma had been the one to dob her in to the department and that was how she'd lost Tegan and she couldn't trust anyone, they were all shits to her even her family.

I looked at my doll's wool hair that Aunty Jacinta had sewed on and made into two little plaits, they were so neat and perfect, tied with thin red ribbon.

When I look at my doll now I remember all this exactly like it happened.

I wrote a card to Aunty Jacinta last year and she wrote a card back to me. Here is what she said: 'Dearest Tyler, we missed you this year and we're sorry you couldn't make it back here again for Christmas. Remember, Ty, we think you're wonderful and would love to see you again any time.' On the bottom of the card was a little arrow pointing to the back where she'd written her phone number and her small writing saying: 'If you ever need to ring me for anything at all, here's the number.' Mum already had that number in the phone book, but Aunty Jacinta must have forgotten. I put the card in my box. I called my doll Calypso. It's just a nice word.

If I had a bike I would of written about that instead.

On Saturday mornings early my mum says I'm allowed to watch cartoons then she goes back into her room. When I peek in as I go past I see an orange shawl over the lamp and a bare foot sticking out of the bed from under the doona. It is Shane's foot, he has a snake tattoo on his ankle. Do you like my tattoo? he said once, lifting up his foot to show me. I said didn't it hurt? and he said yep it sure did. He made me read out the words under the snake and said and don't you forget it, that's the truth, babe.

If you get something written on your skin it's like you imagine yourself blank like a piece of paper, ready for words, but the bones in Shane's ankle bumped up underneath so the letters were crooked. The snake had fangs that were much too big, like a cartoon snake, when they open their mouths their jaw goes right back and the fangs fill the screen and that's impossible. The person they're attacking starts running in midair without going anywhere and first you hear bongo drums and then the noise they're supposed to make when they run really fast.

One thing about the early Saturday cartoons is that sometimes they show the old ones about the cat chasing the mouse. He makes up all these plans to get the mouse but never gets him, then they wreck the house again, running over and over again past the same lamp and the same chair. Sometimes the cat or the coyote gets big red sticks of dynamite and it always happens that they get it wrong and the dynamite blows up their head. Anyone knows you wouldn't survive that but they do. They just shake their heads, which have gone black like someone's dropped a packet of black powder onto the floor and it's split open, then suddenly they're back to normal. They can still run so fast they're a blur.

Live fast die young leave a pretty corpse is what Shane's tattoo says. A corpse is a body like on NCIS. I don't know how you'd stay pretty if you were dead. I watch the cartoons listening for when Shane gets up so I can run and get dressed because I don't like being just in my pyjamas when he's here. It just feels funny.

My birthday today. I got my present from my grandma. As soon as I saw it I knew it wasn't the tin. It was a long plastic packet of coloured pencils all different colours but when I coloured with them it wasn't the same. With Georgia's Derwents it feels soft when you colour and it goes on dark and strong. These pencils feel gritty like there's sand in them and no matter how hard you press the colour isn't very good. Say thank you to your grandma, said my mum, for your lovely pencils. Grandma said they're just what she wanted, aren't they, Tyler?

Mum said that next year I can have a party and we

can go to Lollypops Fun Centre. Ellie said that place is for preschoolers, and Mum said well, Maccas then. We had a birthday afternoon tea because Ellie couldn't stay home for dinner, she had a shift at Subway till 9.30. She whispered to me in the kitchen sorry, Tyler we'll do something good next year, just you and me, don't worry. I said I didn't care because I had cupcakes at school today. Shane wasn't there tonight because Grandma doesn't know about him yet. Mum says she'll introduce them when the time's right. She says Grandma always interferes and wrecks her chances when it's none of her business so don't tell her yet. Ellie asked her why not and she said first Shane has to get his parole period out of the way and get his gold star for staying clean. Maybe that's why Shane comes over to our place to have a shower and get changed. Much later when I was in bed Ellie came in and woke me up and said come into my room. We lay in her bed and she opened a bag from the mall and inside were two little mirror disco balls and two torches. We put batteries in and shone the lights on the mirror balls and sparkling dots went everywhere, all around the corners of the room, spinning. It was like we were floating in the solar system. It was lovely and warm in Ellie's bed.

Thank you for making the cupcakes today, Mrs Carlyle. It was great when everyone sang.

My mum says she is going to have a new job. Centrelink is running it and it is sewing. She is good at sewing and she already has the overlocker Aunty Jacinta gave her to make tracksuit pants and tops two years ago.

It is very heavy and she has to lift it up onto the kitchen table. Ellie asks her what she's sewing and Mum says designer things. She says it is support to start her own small business.

She shows me a pattern and it is not clothes, it's a doll. Sort of like a doll anyway. Like a prep kid's drawing, just a round soft shape with big eyes and two useless little arms sticking out the side. Mum has rolls of felt and soft velvet, stretchy fur material for the clothes. The dolls are called <u>Glamour Plushies</u>.

Designer plush toys, Mum says reading from her pattern page. They're just for fun. I'm going to sell them in that shop with the cushions and teak furniture in the mall, that Asian one.

Are they the scissors? is all Ellie says. The ones that cost forty-five bucks?

Mum says I told you I would pay you back so lose the attitude. She lines up material on the table and Ellie just turns away rolling her eyes.

Mum tells me the scissors are just for special sewing, not for my school stuff or craft things. She says that will wreck them. There is a special tag that gets sewn onto the dolls when they're finished with a card tied on it that says: 'Glamour Plushies are soft, loveable critters that teach us that beauty is only skin-deep. When you adopt one of these adorable soft monsters you are showing your warm-hearted side, a valuable lesson presented by cutely irresistible toys designed and created with great care.' Mum says you will have to help me round the house more, Tyler, so I can get my first order finished for the assessment. I have to make twelve.

So I cook the chicken with the simmer sauce while she cuts out the pieces and says we will eat dinner on our laps tonight so I can leave the overlocker and all my work on the table OK? And I say OK even though we always eat dinner on our laps anyway because Mum is hooked on Survivor.

The stuff for the Glamour Plushies takes up all the room on the table so I have to do my project on the glories of Ancient Greece on my bed after dinner. It's hard to write neatly.

Mum hears me snipping and rustling when she comes down the hall to her room and calls out they better not be the good scissors.

They're not. They're the plastic ones that don't cut. Pictures stuck down with the glue that doesn't stick, coloured in with the pencils that don't colour. Sorry, Mrs Carlyle.

Mum nearly finished two whole dolls today when I got home from school. She said the overlocker doesn't really work properly on the felt so she's worked out how to do the blanket stitch by hand. The dolls have big round eyes and little mouths like cats or big open mouths with teeth and they stick their arms straight out the side like they're running towards you afraid. Out of like a fire or away from a scary thing. They are not dolls, they are more like cartoon monsters. Ellie was doing her homework in her room and I went in there. Her room is nice and she bought some curtains for herself at Spotlight and a hot pink mosquito net. I looked at Ellie's homework which is so hard because she is in Year 10. It was science and she had written, red blood cells plus white blood cells plus platelets plus water equals blood. There was a picture of platelets and they looked like biscuits. When I get to high school I want to do art in the art room where they have easels. I saw them when we went to Ellie's school for parent-teacher. You stand up and paint and they have huge pieces of paper you're allowed to use, as many as you like. And also a pottery wheel. It's those things that make me want to go to the secondary school even though there's hundreds and hundreds of kids there. I get worried I might forget where my locker is in all those corridors. You get a locker with a combination so that only you can open it. Maybe the other kids want to steal your stuff. You would never know who because there are so many kids there is no way a teacher would notice that or even remember everyone's names. Ellie says she just does the subjects that are going to get her good marks, not art, so that she can do something at TAFE or uni. That is why she works part time too, to save all her money. When she and Mum fight Mum says set your sister a good example, and Ellie says I'm setting her the best example I can, which is how to get the fuck out of here.

When we went back into the lounge room for dinner Shane was there. He said here they both are. How are you, Tyler babe? All the cans of beer he has brought are stacked in the fridge when I get out the cheese for the spaghetti. He is in a mean mood I can tell because even though he is smiling his mouth is wrong.

He picks one of Mum's dolls out of the box and looks at it and says you've got to be fucken kidding me.

People pay forty bucks for these says my mum without looking at him, and he laughs and says jeez they saw you coming, didn't they. She just keeps sewing the hair on one of her dolls and says you wait.

When I go to bed I hear him and Mum laughing and bumping into the walls as they come down the hall and my mum sounds happy but it makes the stones feeling come back to my stomach. I must have fallen asleep because I feel a hand on my shoulder shaking me and I come awake and my stomach is squeezing like when you're sick. It is Ellie and I feel her hair brush my face as she leans over me and says get up and come and sleep in my room. I say why and she whispers just come on.

In her bed she lets me have the purple heart-shaped pillow. She shows me a little smooth stone in a box she puts under the pillow and I ask her what it's for and she says bad dreams.

I didn't know Ellie has bad dreams too. Sometimes

I dream of a wolf. He's coming for me and his eyes are on fire and he's looking everywhere for me but he can't find me. I don't tell Ellie about this but I say sometimes I feel like I have a stone inside my stomach. Ellie doesn't say anything for a while then she says, hey, what are those pencils called that you like? I tell her Derwents and she says we'll get those, you wait.

Today we did mammals. Mrs Carlyle said she got a puppy once that was homesick leaving its mother and it cried. She said she wrapped up an old clock inside an old fur collar she had and tucked it into the puppy's basket with a hot-water bottle. The puppy thought the clock ticking was its mother's heart beating and the fur was her warm furry coat next to it. It seemed like a mean trick but Mrs Carlyle said soon the puppy went to sleep and learned to sleep by itself after that. She said it seems cruel but all animals have to learn that and some leave their parents the day they are born, but not mammals because they have to drink milk. That puppy used to like to sleep in the laundry basket full of dirty clothes. When the bell rang she said, whoops, we forgot to do our worksheets, all I've ended up doing is telling you stories because you are such good listeners.

That puppy thought the clock and the fur and the hot-water bottle was his mum. And maybe the clothes in the clothes basket had a smell that made him feel better. The Plushie dolls are supposed to make you feel warm-hearted too so maybe people will buy them to cuddle like a puppy. Birds like budgies can't be cuddled but they must still know you love them. Ellie says we used to have a cat when Dylan and Zac were still here before I was born but it ran away. Ellie says, I don't blame it.

My mum is still sewing the Plushies. She says she has a deadline and she has to prove she can do it so she'll be accepted on the job-creation program. She said if Shane thinks he's so shit-hot why doesn't he fix her car and do something useful? Shane is nearly living at our place now and she said if he thinks all he has to do is turn up with pizzas and five weekly DVDs he's got another think coming. But then when he comes she goes quickly into her room and comes out with perfume on.

While she is in there Shane beckons at me and when I go over he leans down close to me and whispers I've got something for you but don't tell the others, hold out your hand. He gives me a Mars Bar. His voice is so different when he is telling a secret. It is all soft and like you're best friends and I want to believe everything he tells me. He says don't tell Ellie because she will get jealous. Next time I might put it under your pillow so always check when you go to bed OK? In case I've left a surprise for you. Then when Mum walks back in again he says shhh, here she comes and I can't help it, I smile. I hide the Mars Bar in my bag.

Ellie did a magic thing tonight. Mum had the five

Plushies she had finished laid out on the table and she was painting their lips red like in the photo and Ellie said do you want a cup of tea? Mum was just sitting there not saying anything and I realised she had stopped painting and was scratching at her hair like it was itchy just scratching and pulling not answering. Shane was in the living room watching TV and Mum was just sitting there with her chin tucked down all hunched and sad with the dolls lined up. Her hand scratching harder and harder in her hair. I felt like when I turn the key in my music box until it's really tight and if you keep turning one more time it will snap and break, just one more twist. But Ellie came over very quietly and looked down at the monster dolls that were meant to make you feel warm-hearted. They all had big black eyes that just stared and I could tell Mum was thinking they looked creepy or dead and it's true they did.

Ellie put a brush in the white paint and put a little dot of white in the dolls' eyes. I don't know how she did it but it changed everything. It was like a little speck of shine. I heard Mum sigh then her hand came down and felt around for her cigarettes. I felt loose again like remembering that inside the music box the ballerina is waiting to dance to the whole song and it will just get slower and calmer all the way to the end.

Just before when I was going to bed Mum said let's have a secret, you don't have to go to school tomorrow, Tyler. I will ring up and tell them you are sick and you can stay here and help me finish the Plushies. It is the same as when Shane leans down and whispers, grown-ups can make their voices go all soft and excited like it's a big special secret to share just with you, they know just how to make kids feel happy but it's never what you think.

I felt the stones in my stomach because I remembered that tomorrow is the first orientation day for Grade 6s to go over to the senior campus to visit but I just said yes. Mum still has five dolls to make and she said she will show me how to do the blanket stitch.

I woke up in the night and I saw someone was standing in my doorway and at first I thought it was my mum. Then I heard a sniff and I got a shock because it was Shane. When I said what? he pretended he'd been sleepwalking and said sorry, wrong room.

Ellie was mad at Mum today when she went off to school. She said you're supposed to have a doctor's certificate if you're sick and Mum said she has a temperature so mind your own business. Ellie said is Shane going to be hanging round all day? and Mum said of course not he's going to his job with the house painters and Ellie said he'd better. Mum got really angry and said who are you to talk, you've got that hopeless bloke who can't do anything better than work at a takeaway and Ellie said if you mean Luke he's store manager and he's going to uni next year. Her voice was trembling but I never see Ellie cry. Mum just said oh, uni, is it? That's typical you'd pick him, now you can both be up yourselves together. When she gets angry she just says things that don't make any sense. Ellie just said he's a smart nice guy who likes me so no wonder you don't get it. And since your useless boyfriend ruined your car it's Luke that's been driving me home, so thank goodness someone's there to make sure I make it home OK, not that you'd care about that.

Mum went red as a beetroot and said just get out and get yourself to school so you can do what you're good at and that's show off.

Ellie just looked at her and said is that the best you can do? Like she was tired. On her way out she said to me, use the phone I got for you to text me at school if anything goes wrong OK? I said like what? and she said if you get the stones feeling.

Shane was still in bed when Mum got onto the phone to my school after Ellie had gone. She could swap straight away from shouting at Ellie to putting on a phone voice. I had to unpick one of the Plushies and put more stuffing in when I finished because its arms were too floppy. We sewed them in front of the TV and Mum kept going back to check the instructions to make sure we were doing them right even though she's made five already. She said you don't understand, Tyler, it just keeps slipping out of my brain. We watched The Morning Show and Dr Phil while we sewed. Shane went out at lunchtime but he didn't say anything about going to work. By four o'clock we'd finished six more Plushies and my fingers were all pricked and tingly but the dolls all had different personalities now because we were getting better at adding little bits and making them different. Their arms looked like they were about to hug you rather than sticking out straight because they were scared. Mum laid them out in a line when they were finished and said you put the little dot in their eyes, Ty, my hand is shaking too much. So I did Ellie's magic trick and the Plushies stopped being scary and all of a sudden looked alive. Mum will take them to the shop tomorrow while I am at school and maybe somebody will buy one who wants a cutely irresistible toy.

I was in bed when Ellie came home and she woke me up. She said do you want some of this meatball sub? and I said no then she said, well, you can sleep in my bed if you like. I said I wanted to sleep in my own bed and she said, well, how about I get in with you.

When I made room she sat down and I whispered who is Luke? and she laughed a bit and whispered back oh, just this guy. I asked is he good-looking? and she said I think he is, I'll show you a photo of him tomorrow on my phone. I think she was going to tell me more but then she stopped and said hey, did Shane do or say anything weird today? I said he just sits with me when the cartoons are on and she said does he get you to sit in his lap? If he does anything like that you come and tell me straight away. I said, why not Mum? and I could see Ellie's face go sad and tired and she said no, just tell me.

Ellie said Zac and Dylan went to live with other families because they had police records when they were just kids and they ran away thinking they wanted to live with their dad but they didn't really because their dad was hopeless, but Tegan went because of Ian, Mum's old boyfriend before Gary. Mum had a screaming fight with child protection and said everyone was lying but it didn't stop Tegan going. She got taken away and Mum didn't stop it. I felt the heavy heavy weight in my stomach as she whispered. Like when you sit in the bath and all the water drains out. Ellie said you have to be careful of him and I said but I'm just a kid and Ellie said that's why, Ty, that's why.

There wasn't much room in my bed when she'd squeezed in and I smelled her hair which smelled like the bread in Subway and I said that's why you're saving up, isn't it, so you can go too and she didn't answer for so long I thought she must've started going to sleep. Then I heard her say Tyler, she might have left me but I'm not leaving you, not ever.

I asked Mum if she would drive me to the mall today. Georgia told me at school that at the art supply shop there they have Derwents and she thought you can buy them just one at a time. Mum drove me there and it was a bit scary driving in the car because she had to keep revving it up at the traffic lights to keep it from conking out. What

Ellie said is true, it's not going well since Shane fixed it. Mum said never mind, Tyler, it's still good having a guy around the place, isn't it, and I said yes and she said it makes you feel safe, doesn't it, and I said yes again. She said he's going to be on the straight and narrow now but he's had his problems like all of us.

At the mall she said she would meet me in half an hour and I went to the art supply shop and I had enough money to buy five pencils. I couldn't decide which colours I wanted first. Finally I picked out my five. Scarlet Lake, Oriental Blue, Deep Cadmium, Lemon Yellow and Cloud Blue. If I did a picture of a blue budgie it would be Cloud Blue and Iced Blue with extra grey on the feathers. When I close my eyes I can see exactly how that drawing would look, like the picture I did of the running horse I drew in science and the teacher said where did you copy this and I said I didn't copy it, it just came out of my head. It was Mr Godfrey and he said are you saying you did this freehand? I said yes, even though I wasn't sure what freehand was, and he said OK then let's see you draw one now on the whiteboard, in a voice like I was in trouble. I felt angry instead of nervous because he didn't believe me so I just started drawing a horse with two huge wings coming out of its back, right to the edge of the whiteboard. He didn't say sorry for not believing you he just said well then, I think I've found the student who's going to decorate the board for parent–teacher night. Except for Mrs Carlyle I never want to tell the teachers if I like something because this is what happens, they use it to make you do something they want.

I think sometimes about what you would have to do to be an artist, for example how would you make money. My pencils have <u>student quality</u> written on the packet but the Derwent pencils are for real artists and that is why they're special. I would feel special and proud to have them, like when Aunty Jacinta wrote in her letter, we think you're wonderful.

I said to Mum I wanted to look at our Plushies in the gift shop and first she didn't want to. She said she'd be too embarrassed and the lady would think she was a loser, hanging round looking at them only a few days after she'd dropped them off. She said it would be more professional to stay away until she got a phone call or something. But I wanted to see what I had made for sale in a real shop.

Finally we went up there and looked in the display window which looked so nice with embroidered cushions and wooden carved elephants and Mum said it's not here, it was right here in front of that basket and she's taken it out.

Her voice had gone quiet and far off and she was chewing on her lips and breathing hard. She said she must have only left it there to shut me up for a while, it was the good one I made, Tyler, with the stripy shirt. I said I want to go in and see if they're inside sitting in a basket or something and Mum said no, don't, we're wasting our time here. I thought about all that sewing and Centrelink giving Mum the test and just then the lady who owned the shop saw us and her face changed when she saw Mum and Mum said come on we're out of here.

But the lady came running out calling Mum's name and said I was about to call you and tell you. Mum said are they inside? and I could tell how much she tried to keep her voice normal. Because my little girl here helped me make those things, if you didn't want them you should have just said. But the lady said they're not inside, they're all gone. We both just looked at her and she said it's amazing the whole lot have sold out in three days, I was going to ring you to tell you to come in and I'd pay you.

We didn't say anything we just followed her into the shop and she had a receipt and an envelope for Mum there with her name already on it and she said I'll take as many as you can make. Mum just nodded and grabbed my arm really tightly and steered me out of the shop. We went down the escalators and she opened the envelope without saying anything and bought two Krispy Kreme doughnuts and we went back to the car and got in and we still hadn't said a word. As she was trying to start the car I was thinking that I could have bought another pencil for the same price as my doughnut and the car revved then rattled like it was laughing at us and then stopped.

We sat there with sugar all round our mouths then Mum looked down at the envelope in her lap and tears dripped on it. She kept crying and shaking and not even wiping the tears and snot away then she took out thirty dollars and said Tyler, this is for you, this is your share.

Today Mum went to do the supermarket shopping and I was home watching TV when the phone rang and someone said is Shane Talbot there, please? He was asleep but Mum says never tell a stranger on the phone that anyone is asleep so I just asked if I could take a message and the person said please tell him someone from the Community Offender Services Office needs to speak with him. When I told Shane that he got straight out of bed and pushed past me and just listened on the phone saying yes, yes, sure thing, yes. When he hung up he said to me Tyler, do you like to do your friends favours?

I said yes. I didn't really know what else to say. So many of Shane's questions you can't really answer, like he'll say wassup, Tyler baby? And, all good eh, Tyler? But there's nothing really to say to those questions.

But I said yes and he smiled and said that's good, because you can do a little favour for me. It's a simple thing. It's something so simple you won't believe it.

I was watching him smiling and nodding at me and even though his voice was friendly his hand was in his mouth and I could see his teeth biting the bleeding cuticle down the side of his thumbnail all the time he was talking. The stone in my stomach was squeezing and pressing, sending a taste up into my mouth. Not a taste. Like when you have an Easter egg and the foil gets bitten onto one of your fillings. Like fingernails on the blackboard.

I said what is the favour? I kept looking at my sandals. I liked them when I got them in Target because they had small pressed-out daisies on the top but now they just looked stupid and babyish. My toes were hanging out over the edge all grubby. I swallowed down the foil taste.

He told me what it was and it's like the words he's saying don't make sense, like they're broken up in a box and I can't start sorting through them to put them back together. And the stone shifts and slips and I feel sweat on my skin because my heart jumps up into the back of my mouth.

He says Tyler, I need you to piss into a cup and give it to me. I know it sounds crazy but it's just a surprise trick I'm playing.

All the muscles go stiff on my face and Shane is smiling so wide his mouth is big and stretched. He says hey, you're blushing. It's just for a surprise. You can't tell anyone.

I say why not Mum? and his face closes up like a window and his lip gets that mean look and he says I thought you were my friend, I thought you would be a good person to ask, because you can keep a secret. But can you, Tyler? I say yes I can. He says you have to do it in a special cup, with a lid. Well, so the piss doesn't spill out and so that I can carry it. I just put the lid on OK?

I say OK again and my mind is picking up one piece, searching, searching for another piece to make sense. And Shane looks at the time on his phone and says do you need to go now, Tyler baby? Because if you can go right now for me that would be great and I can get the surprise going.

I get up and take the cup, walk out with my jigsaw-box head and my foil mouth. Ellie tried to tell me to watch out for him but not for this, not going to the toilet. Not sitting trying to catch the wee that gushes out of me, seeing my white legs jiggling on the toilet seat. I go back and his hand is already stretched out waiting for me with the fingers going come on come on come on. I give him the cup and I see the face he makes when he feels it's warm and I get really small and a thread is pulling through me like I am one of the dolls stitched up tight and stiff.

He says that's perfect, I owe you one, Tyler babe, and he screws on the lid and runs out of the house. I am putting this in my journal for Mrs Carlyle because she said it's good to write about things even if they make us feel ashamed or like we want to cry. Now I don't want to write anymore.

My mum has worked out how to make the overlocker do blanket stitch and she says check this out, girls, I've got a sweatshop going here. She says it's so much quicker now, Tyler, and if you can just help me do the hair and the faces I'll be able to do stacks of them. She has put colour in her hair and it is a red-brown colour. Vermilion plus Burnt Umber. The internet is back on for the computer so Mum says there's no reason why Ellie has to hang round to use the ones in the school library which means I won't be able to stay there with her after school and read Charlie and the Chocolate Factory in the beanbag in the story corner.

This morning Mrs Carlyle said now my dearest 6Cs, I'm going to put this box here on my desk and if anyone would like to take the opportunity to put their journals in so I can read them, I would be so happy and honoured.

I am just waiting after school for Ellie to walk across from the senior campus to come and meet me and there's no one else here so I'm going to put mine in.

I've checked in the box already and it's empty but maybe Mrs Carlyle has already taken the other ones out.

On Monday night and last night I didn't have my journal to write in and it felt strange, like waiting for a phone call with news to tell the person but they don't ring. Now it's Wednesday night. I want to tell Ellie about Shane making me do a wee but just thinking about it makes the stone come up into my chest and neck and it jams my throat shut so I can't talk.

My journal was back inside my work folder this morning and when Mrs Carlyle asked me to stay behind the same thing happened. She said she had to make an appointment for me to be interviewed by someone and I couldn't speak, just shook my head, because my throat felt all squeezed up. She said it's about your journal, Tyler, and I kept shaking my head and she said, your mother ...

I felt everything go blurry then because it would be the police, like what happened with Tegan that Ellie told me about, and I just said flat out no.

She said what are you doing this afternoon? I was meant to go to the mall and wait for Ellie to finish an after-school shift because Mum was going to her Centrelink course so there would be nobody home except Shane. So I said the mall.

Mrs Carlyle said would you like me to give you a lift to the mall then? And I said OK. We walked down the empty corridor to the teachers' car park and it felt really strange. I stopped and she said would you rather I drove you straight home and I said no, not home, and this sounded so stupid but the thought of Shane sitting there watching cartoons made the stones grind together so that I just couldn't move or make myself get into the car. Then Mrs Carlyle was crouching down next to me and she was saying, Tyler, if you could go anywhere now where would you like to go? My voice came back and I said I want to go to your house and see the budgies. It just came out in a rush because it was exactly what I did want.

She was quiet for a minute and then she said right let's do that. That's how I ended up visiting Mrs Carlyle at her house. She had a great front door with a big knocker on it like a hand and you had to hold the hand to make it knock back and forth, tapping on the door. I said I love that and she said so do I. We had Milo and biscuits in her kitchen and then she showed me the spot in the back garden where the budgies lived. It was not like I imagined, I thought they would be in a little cage, but it was a big space with a net around it. It took up almost the whole garden. Mrs Carlyle said she wanted them to have an aviary because she didn't like to think of birds not being able to fly around. The nest inside was made out of a plastic milk bottle cut open and stuffed with soft hay and feathers just like she told us. She said the mother bird is in there, Tyler, so we'd better not disturb her. But it means there are eggs and I haven't forgotten my promise to you.

We sat on a seat in her garden under a tree and I wished I had one of those too. She said do you think we should ring your mother and let her know where you are, Tyler? and I said no, she won't be home. I said if it was OK she could drop me back at the mall and I would go to meet my sister to get the bus. She said that's Ellie, right? and I felt all hot thinking she had read that in my journal. For a long time we didn't say anything then Mrs Carlyle said I just want to do the right thing by you, Tyler, I just don't know exactly what that is. She reached over and took my hand and said the school rules are so insane, I'll probably get reprimanded by the school board for even bringing you here, it's the department's policy. I felt the stones squeeze up remembering what Ellie had said about the department. I don't want to get taken away I said, and my voice was all stupid and high and squeaky like a cartoon. I won't tell anyone we came here to your place. Mrs Carlyle kept holding on to my hand and said that won't happen, Tyler, but I'm bound by mandatory reporting so I don't have any choice.

And I felt my stomach gulp like I was one of her birds swooping through the air in their big home she had made for them. Their <u>aviary</u>. She said do you trust me, Tyler? and I looked in at the milk bottle nest cut neatly open and tied so carefully onto the post inside and the tray of soft straw and grass she had found for them to use and I said yes. I said if I put my hand into the nest now would the mother bird bite me? And she looked so sad at me and nodded. We fed the birds and then she drove me back to the mall.

I was in our backyard. It was funny but when I'd been at Mrs Carlyle's I'd kind of imagined my backyard to be different. Like it had trees where I could nail up netting in a corner and make a kind of aviary so I wouldn't have to put my bird in a tiny cage. But I'd remembered it wrong and there were no trees. Just bushes next to the fence and the clothesline and the paving. Mum was inside working on finishing off the dolls. On Thursday night she had come home from her Centrelink course with a sort of artist's smock her case worker had given her, she said it's a real tailor's apron for people who work in fabric and she showed Ellie and me the pockets at the front where the scissors and cottons and pincushion went and Shane came in and said well, lookie here it's Doris Day and burst out laughing and Mum stood there for a minute then she laughed too and pulled the apron off and said you're right it's stupid.

I said, Mum, that colour is a Derwent colour and it's called Pale Mint and she just nodded and went into the kitchen. But she had the apron back on today because Shane wasn't here. I was standing looking at the bushes and the fence wondering how I'd remembered them so wrong and thinking about the weekend and I didn't know it but it was the last minute of everything being the same.

Ellie was in her room and I could hear her voice through the window just very softly singing along to the song she loves playing on her iPod, Three Little Birds, she was up to the chorus where the words go cause every little thing is gonna be alright, and then I heard the front door slam and Shane's voice shouting where is she? where the fuck is she? Then Mum shouting what? what? but her voice not angry enough, not enough to stop him, and Shane saying I've had my parole officer on my back and that dumb-arsed brat of yours has fucked everything up for me because she ran and told her fucken teacher. I could hear him going down the hall and I heard his voice say I'll kill her. And Ellie screamed and that's when I ran into the laundry and climbed into the clothes basket. It is a big cane basket with all the week's dirty washing in it and I pulled some clothes over me and lay still. Everyone was screaming now and I thought, all jumbled up, of Mrs Carlyle telling the principal and Aunty Jacinta's phone number folded up in the box on my chest of drawers and how my mobile phone was lying on my bed with a flat battery so I couldn't of rung the police anyway. My whole stomach was full of stones now gritting heavy together and I shut my eyes and thought Cloud Blue Kingfisher Blue Oriental Blue Iced Blue Prussian Blue Indigo. I heard Mum say she's not here and Shane said bullshit and Mum said OK, OK, calm down and her voice was all scared and hopeless and I knew she wasn't going to be any good to me. I just hated her then and I went to burrow down deeper into the clothes. I felt something sharp sticking into my hip as I curled up my legs tight and I put my hand down very carefully without making a sound and felt around. It was something hard and plastic in the pocket of the shirt my mum had worn the night before to her class and I could just see it, a square white badge that said Student of the Week. I thought Grey Green Sea Green Light Sand French Grey Rose Pink and my breath was coming out funny and then I got up out of the basket and even though my legs felt like jelly I walked into the living room.

Right, said Shane when he saw me. You. I've breached my parole conditions now thanks to you, you interfering little bitch.

I looked at Mum and she just stood there in her green apron and I could see her shoulders hunching and her face closing up and Ellie stepped in front of me and said good, because I already called the police, and Shane turned around to her and grabbed her and threw her hard against the wall and I heard her head bang against the plaster and it's not true what happens in cartoons, people don't leave a person-shaped hole in the wall when they hit it.

She falls on the floor, my sister. But as soon as she does she stands up again grabbing onto a chair and Mum says in a voice like something far away, don't touch my kids.

Shane turns back to her and his mouth goes scary and he says I should have known, everyone told me I was crazy to get involved with you. Everyone. They all know you're fucked in the head.

Mum is like one of the dolls without enough stuffing, loose and floppy, her hand on the bench to help her stand up. She's going to fall over and then we will have to see what he does to us. All the things she doesn't see, she will see them now but she will be too weak to stand up.

I feel Ellie behind me now, I smell her Oil of Olay and her lipgloss. My sister.

And this one, Shane says pointing behind me at her. This little prickteaser here, she's going to turn out just like her mother, that one. Just like you. Five bastard kids to five different blokes, can't look after any of em. And too dumb to charge for it.

Mum is still hunched up with her mouth open like she can't make it say anything. She'll be a chip off the old block, he says to Mum. Ellie doesn't say anything and I know why. I can hear her in my head, saying Tyler, let him just spew it out, don't say anything or he will hurt us. I hear her voice like when she is singing in her room, small but clear.

Mum turns and stares at us, Ellie and me. Then words come out of her mouth again, tired and cold. You'd better get out of here now. I think she means us to run and get away but I can't move with Shane watching us, holding us frozen there.

Look at her, says Shane, pointing at Ellie. Crawling up to me. She hates you. Don't you, Ellie?

I turn around and Ellie shakes her head no no no. Tears fill up her eyes. Mum just stares at Ellie and I feel everything rock for a minute, back and forth. Then Mum flinches and blinks like something has just brushed across her face.

I mean it, out right now or else, she says. But she's not saying it to Ellie, she's saying it to him. A quiet voice. And she's reaching into her apron pocket and she brings out the big silver scissors, the good scissors.

You've got to be fucken joking, says Shane, laughing like she's just said something stupid. On the bench is the big square knife and he slides it into his hand and now the stones in my stomach are so heavy I just want to sink down and sit on the floor because he does it so easily, you can see he's not scared at all of just sticking it in her.

I'm warning you, he says, you're making me have to defend myself. His wrist comes up and he's pointing to the small blue tattoo on his neck, just a blue and blurry smudge. See this? he says. That means I done this before and believe me, bitch, I got no problems doing it again.

He did that himself, I hear Ellie say inside my head. He's never been in jail. What sort of loser boasts about jail, and it isn't even true. Sad bastard with homemade tattoos. I'm right behind you, Ty. Right here.

I warned you too, says our mother and she steps forward with a little sigh as if it's all finished for her and she wants him to do it, but it's like my mum's arm has got strong hauling up the sewing machine every night and lifting all those rolls of material onto the table, she swings quick and easy like she's pushing the car door closed then she steps back again and the scissors are buried in his stomach, just with the handles sticking out.

Shane looks down amazed. Here's the part I don't understand, Mrs Carlyle, he could have still stabbed us all to death then but he didn't even look up. He just started crying. Then he sat on the floor with his head down and held his stomach crying and my mum said, Ellie, time to phone the police for real now. And she wasn't like a doll anymore. Someone had come along and put the white dots into her eyes and they were bright as black glittering glass and her mouth was like the line you cut in the felt, one hard snip straight across the pattern, across the exact right spot. She held out one arm and Ellie went into it.

Look, Mrs Carlyle, I am writing this in Prussian Blue. Guess what Ellie got me for Christmas. Yes! It was the Derwents and all the blue ones are still my favourites. When you told us to write the journal you were still my teacher but I missed the last two weeks of final term when I went up to Aunty Jacinta's place after all this happened. My mum asked me where did I want to go and I said her place and Mum didn't even argue, she said I think you're right, we all need a holiday. When I opened my present there at Christmas and saw it was the pencils I nearly cried and Aunty Jacinta showed me something I'd never noticed before. She said, look at that drawing of the bridge on the tin, Ty. The artist has drawn it so carefully you can see how all those stones fit together to make that arch over the water, and then she opened the tin and said, look, on every single one of your new pencils they have stamped the word <u>artist</u>.

I only realised later that next year, when school starts again, I will be in secondary school across the road so you won't be my teacher anymore. But when you gave us the books you said it didn't matter where we started and finished and maybe the journal will never be finished but it doesn't matter. I kept writing mine these holidays so that you will know you were right. I have been thinking and thinking about when we went to your house to see the budgies and they ate seed out of your hand and you said, Tyler, our true friends never ask us to do favours as a test and you looked so sad. I want to say I hope you are not sad now because you helped me and I tried to be brave like you said and now I think I'm going good.

I still remember where you live. I'm going to put this in your letterbox. I hope that is OK. I hope you are still living there. If your budgie's eggs hatch please will you call one of the babies Alicia. One day I will get an aviary and then I will come and get her, Mrs Carlyle. That's my promise.

Acknowledgements

To name just a few people I am indebted to, thank you David Dore, Robin and Margie Hemley, Hal Wake, Kate Rotherham, Terry Jaensch, Hannie Rayson, Yiyun Li, Willy Vlautin and David Francis. I have experienced nothing but support and warmth from those who make Melbourne the city it is for a writer from the sticks, namely Michael Williams and the staff at the Wheeler Centre, Steve Grimwade, and of course Henry Rosenbloom at Scribe, and Ian See. Thanks to those stubborn and dedicated people who have given some of these stories a home in a time of huge uncertainty for literary journals, magazines and anthologies. And, as always, thanks to my terrific publisher and editor Aviva Tuffield — still loyally in the car I seem to be driving, still holding the thermos.